A CHEAP SHOT

"Get him, Bert! Get him!" some of the miners shouted.

Bert snorted like a bull and tried to grab Longarm and crush him. Ducking and retreating, Longarm bought a few precious minutes by managing to elude the miner's charges. But the bells were still ringing in his head when Bert aimed another kick at his groin. Longarm managed to grab the miner's boot with both hands and heave it upward. Bert slammed down on his back so hard that the wind gushed from his lungs. Longarm didn't wait for him to recover. He dropped on the man's chest and sledged him four or five times in the face, breaking Bert's nose and opening a wicked gash across his cheek . . .

DON'T MISS THESE
ALL-ACTION WESTERN SERIES
FROM THE BERKLEY PUBLISHING GROUP

THE GUNSMITH by J. R. Roberts
Clint Adams was a legend among lawmen, outlaws, and ladies. They called him . . . the Gunsmith.

LONGARM by Tabor Evans
The popular long-running series about U.S. Deputy Marshal Long—his life, his loves, his fight for justice.

SLOCUM by Jake Logan
Today's longest-running action Western. John Slocum rides a deadly trail of hot blood and cold steel.

BUSHWHACKERS by B. J. Lanagan
An action-packed series by the creators of Longarm! The rousing adventures of the most brutal gang of cutthroats ever assembled—Quantrill's Raiders.

TABOR EVANS

LONGARM

AND THE BRANDED BEAUTY

J

JOVE BOOKS, NEW YORK

LONGARM AND THE BRANDED BEAUTY

A Jove Book / published by arrangement with
the author

PRINTING HISTORY
Jove edition / May 1998

The Penguin Putnam Inc. World Wide Web site address is
http://www.penguinputnam.com

ISBN: 0-515-12278-5

A JOVE BOOK®
Jove Books are published by The Berkley Publishing Group,
a member of Penguin Putnam Inc.,
200 Madison Avenue, New York, New York 10016.
JOVE and the "J" design are trademarks
belonging to Jove Publications, Inc.

PRINTED IN THE UNITED STATES OF AMERICA

10 9 8 7 6 5 4 3 2 1

LONGARM

AND THE
BRANDED BEAUTY

Chapter 1

"Marshal Long, are you sitting here in this first-class coach stone sober and telling me that you're really a *friend* of Miss Stella Vacarro?" the Auburn, California, banker wanted to know as their train struggled over Donner Pass. He shook his head in amazement. "I . . . I just can't believe it! That woman is—"

"I think you'd better not say any more," Longarm warned, his voice taking on a hard edge. "I said that she was my friend and that the reason I'm on this train is to attend her wedding. I don't figure I need to defend my reasons . . . or her name and reputation."

The heavyset banker in his fifties, whose name was Ed Haley, expelled a deep sigh and replied, "Marshal Long, with all due respect, perhaps you don't know Miss Vacarro very well. She has had an extremely colorful and sordid past. Did you know, for example, that she once worked on the Comstock Lode as a whore?"

Longarm glanced out the window at the peaks of the towering Sierras. They were almost to the long tunnel that ran under Donner Pass and that had cost so many Chinese lives

1

less than a decade ago when the Central Pacific Railroad had blasted its way through this great range of mountains.

"Yes," Longarm replied. "I did know that."

"All right," Haley said. "Did you also know that she became a madam of one of the biggest whorehouses in Virginia City? An establishment so notorious that the Comstock Lode undertakers voted her their favorite citizen!"

"It was a very rough time," Longarm declared. "They never did have a decent marshal up in Virginia City. I was there three or four times trying to help out, but . . . well, you have to have local support. Maybe you didn't know that Stella also gave a tremendous amount of money to the orphanage, disabled miners, and their widows, as well as to St. Mary of the Mountains Catholic Church."

"A real hypocrite, that woman. She was only trying to keep from having the decent folks of Virginia City run her and her whores out of town . . . if not worse."

"Listen," Longarm said, "I don't mean to sound rough, but I've heard about as much as I care to hear from you."

"Just one more thing you should know," the banker said, "and that's that Stella Vacarro knifed a man to death on the Comstock with a silver stiletto. She also slashed another man's face in Auburn about two years ago."

"I know all about the killing," Longarm said, "including that it was ruled self-defense."

"Probably because Stella paid off the judge and jury," the banker growled. "Marshal Long, this wedding is the talk of California. And for the life of me, I cannot imagine what kind of an evil spell that Vacarro woman has cast upon young Noah Huffington. Do you realize that he had been previously engaged to a fine young woman of good character and that Noah was even going to start his own *ministry*?"

2

"No," Longarm admitted, "I did not."

"Everyone in Auburn, including Noah's father, was delighted. Miss Carole Clark came from a very well-respected, though not wealthy, family. She was a perfect match for Noah. When they walked down the street together they turned the heads of everyone in town. That couple just *looked* as if they were a marriage made in heaven."

"But Noah Huffington broke the engagement and chose to marry Miss Vacarro instead?"

"That's right! Who could figure it!" The banker turned livid. "Why would any young man in his right mind jilt a fine lady like Miss Clark in order to marry a . . . ."

"Don't say it," Longarm warned, balling up his fists. "I don't want to smash your face, but I will if you slander Miss Vacarro anymore."

The banker jumped to his feet and began to shout, causing everyone in their passenger coach to stop talking and to stare. "Marshal, if you lay a hand on me, I'll have your badge! And how you can defend that evil woman and support this wedding defies all logic and every moral code given to man by the Lord!"

Longarm had to struggle to keep from jumping up and attacking the sanctimonious banker. It took all his resolve to simply say, "Doesn't the Bible say something about not judging one another lest we be judged?"

Haley, jowls quivering with self-righteousness, stomped away muttering imprecations. Longarm stood up, stretched to his full impressive height, and gave the other passengers his most benign smile. "Ladies and gentlemen," he announced, "I apologize for this bit of unpleasantness."

"That's all fine for you to say," a thin, nervous little

3

woman across the aisle hissed, "but how *can* you defend someone like that awful Vacarro woman!"

"Because I was taught that God forgives the sinner."

"But not the sin," the woman said, "and Stella Vacarro is not only a murderess, but she has broken up a union that would have been holy."

Longarm had had enough of this talk. This was not the only coach on the train. Maybe he could find one where the people were a whole lot more tolerant. Stella had saved Longarm's life once, at no small personal risk. And she *was* an extremely generous person with both her time and her money. Longarm himself had listened to the priest in Virginia City relate how in times of crisis, whether it be sickness, a mine fire, or a cave-in, Stella was always one of the first to arrive to help and the last to leave. Not only was the woman smart, tough, and beautiful, she was a Good Samaritan. And *that,* Longarm was quite sure, was undoubtedly the reason why Noah Huffington had lost his heart to Stella and chosen to break his highly popular engagement with Miss Carole Clark.

Longarm started to reach down and grab his bag with the thought of leaving the coach when the train suddenly plunged into the Donner Tunnel. In preparation for this, the porters had already lighted the kerosene lamps at each end of the coach, but their glow was feeble and flickering, barely enough to keep the interior of the coach from turning inky black.

Longarm sat down, deciding that this was no time to be fumbling around in the coach. Maybe he'd just keep his seat and ask the porter for a newspaper. Perhaps the *Reno Gazette* or the *Sacramento Bee*. Either would be fine. And in a few more hours, the train would be rolling into Auburn and he wouldn't need to put up with these judgmental people any longer. One thing this encounter had shown him, however, was that he had better not expect a happy wedding in Auburn.

The Donner Tunnel was long, and it would take almost five minutes for the laboring steam engines to pull the train through and then start on down the western slopes of the Sierras. Longarm closed his eyes and chewed his cheroot thoughtfully. It was too bad, he decided, that the people in Auburn were so offended by a wedding that he had come so far to attend. But given that Noah Huffington's father was Abe Huffington, one of the wealthiest and most powerful men in northern California, perhaps it was naive of Longarm not to have expected the public outrage that he was now hearing. After all, it was common knowledge that Abe Huffington was almost certain to win the next election and become California's new governor. The man was said to be a vigorous campaigner as well as an exceptionally good public speaker. Given what Longarm had heard so far on this train, he could only imagine how much damage this marriage would cause to Abe's promising political career.

The darkness deepened, kept at bay only because of the flickering lamps at each end of the coach. Since Longarm was seated near the middle of the coach, he couldn't see his hand in front of his face. Suddenly, the lamp up at the front of the coach went out. Longarm thought nothing of it until the lantern at the back of the coach suddenly went out too. Even this did not cause much of a stir among the passengers because the coach was drafty and it seemed likely that both lamps had accidentally expired. But when Longarm heard a woman scream and then heard shouts punctuated by a shotgun's blast, he knew that he was in the middle of a train robbery.

Longarm wore a .44-caliber Colt inconspicuously strapped under his brown tweed suit coat, butt turned forward. His hand reached for the weapon and it came up smooth and quick. But the coach was as dark as a tomb and there was nothing he could do but sit still and wait for a target.

The tunnel seemed a hundred miles long as the minutes ticked slowly past. Then Longarm heard a man shout, "This is a holdup! We have shotguns and know how to use them! Everyone remove their weapons and throw them into the aisle! Don't throw 'em so hard that they hit the folks seated on the *other* side of the aisle! Just throw 'em easy and no-body will get hurt!"

Longarm tossed his Colt into the aisle. He had no intention of starting a gun battle among these passengers. But he quickly removed the twin-barrel .44-caliber derringer cleverly attached to his Ingersoll watch and chain. Slipping the derringer in between his seat and the wall of the coach, he leaned back and waited to see what would happen next.

"Okay, folks, we're almost through this tunnel and we'd better see everyone's gun resting in the aisle. If we find you're still armed, we'll kill you."

As soon as the man finished speaking, their coach burst into the high mountain sunshine.

"Everyone raise your hands over your heads! We're coming down the aisles and every one of you are going to give us all your money and jewelry."

Longarm ground his teeth in frustration because now he could see that the robber up at the head of the coach was wearing a mask and pressing a shotgun to a young woman's head. Meanwhile, a second masked man was starting down the aisle with a big pillowcase clutched in his fist. From what Longarm could tell, there was another outlaw and hostage holder in the rear of the coach doing the very same thing. Maybe *all* the coaches were being robbed, but Longarm had his doubts. Except for himself, everyone in this coach was well-to-do, with fat wallets and plenty of high-dollar jewelry. Given his lowly marshal's pay, Longarm could never have afforded to ride in this luxurious coach if Stella had not sent him a first-class ticket.

"My dear Marshal Custis Long, indulge yourself," her note had said when it arrived with the tickets. "And be prepared for anything when you arrive in Auburn."

Well, Longarm thought, the question now is if I'll even make it to Auburn.

This was Longarm's reasoning as the masked bag men began to work their way toward the center of the coach. They waved their guns, threatening and scaring the passengers, who were handing over all their rings, necklaces, and other jewelry. No doubt some had had the presence of mind to hide a few jewels or the money from their wallets, but most looked too scared. The robbers were very professional, and because they were all masked, Longarm wouldn't be able to identify them later. All he could say was that they acted like they'd practiced this drill a good many times.

When he reached Longarm, the man with the bag said, "All right, mister, your watch and money. Nice and easy and don't try to be a hero."

Longarm reached inside his coat for his wallet. He had about a hundred dollars in cash and damned if he could spare giving it up, but there wasn't any choice.

"And now your pocket watch."

7

"I don't wear one," Longarm said, trying to look scared out of his mind.

"The watch and chain in my bag *now,* or your brains spattered on the window. Which will it be?"

Longarm removed his watch and gold chain, then tossed them into the bag.

"Good damned choice," the outlaw said with a chuckle as he continued on down the aisle.

Every first-class passenger was fleeced in less than ten minutes. Longarm didn't dare crane his neck around, but he'd have been willing to bet that this robbery had netted these men more than ten thousand in cash and jewelry. Maybe a lot more. No telling if the other coaches or the mail car was also being looted.

"All right, folks," the outlaw called as he and his friends backed to the exits. "It's been a pleasure and we hope to see you again under happier circumstances. Don't try to come after us. We're taking hostages, but we'll let them go after we're sure we aren't being hounded."

The train slowly ground to a halt. Longarm watched through a window as at least five outlaws sprinted for waiting horses. Minutes later, the gang disappeared into the pine forest.

The instant they were gone, Banker Haley charged up the aisle to Longarm's side, face livid as he stood over him. "What kind of a lawman are you anyway! You didn't do a damn thing to stop them! I lost two thousand dollars and a solid gold watch my father left me! I—"

Longarm came out of his seat and grabbed the shouting banker. With a hard twist, he slammed the man down into the seat he'd just left.

"One more word and I'll break your jaw in so many places that you won't even be able to spit!"

The banker paled, and then jumped up and hurried away. Meanwhile, Longarm had turned and raced down the aisle, but he knew that the High Sierra train robbers and their hostages were already long gone.

Chapter 2

When the train finally rolled into Auburn, there was a great deal of consternation and confusion. By then, everyone knew that Longarm was a United States deputy marshal working out of Denver. What they didn't know was that he was on a very well-deserved vacation and had no intention of interfering with the local authorities. Sure, he was plenty angry about the robbery and losing his gold watch and chain as well as his six-gun, but dammit, he *was* on vacation and he was here to attend Stella's wedding.

"Marshal, I don't understand you at all!" an elderly man shouted as they were exiting the train. "First you let them bastards rob us blind, and now you say that you're not even going to lift a hand to catch them sonsabitches!"

"Listen," Longarm said, grabbing the old geezer's arm. "If I'd tried to stop those men, there would have been a bloodbath. A lot of innocent people would have been killed and wounded. And as for going after them, I haven't a horse or a gun or the authority. I'm sure the local marshal will form a posse to track those robbers down quickly."

"Well, what about the two young ladies that they kidnapped?"

Longarm wore a handlebar mustache, and sometimes it actually twitched when he became upset. Like now. "I feel very bad for those women, but the bank robbers did promise to release them unharmed."

"And what if they didn't!"

"If they *didn't*," Longarm growled, "then I'd cancel my vacation and join the manhunt. It's one thing to rob people, another thing to do them harm."

"It's damned obvious to me that you didn't see those two ladies, did you."

"No," Longarm admitted, "I did not. I understand they were taken hostage out of the second-class coach."

"They were pretty," the old man told him. "A couple of young nurses on their way to visit friends in San Francisco. One was Miss Sally Benson; the other was her best friend, Miss Debra Potter."

"I'm sure that they've been set free and we'll find them very soon," Longarm said. "Robbers don't usually kill unless they are trapped and forced to shoot their way out of a fix. That's why I decided that I had no choice but to cooperate."

A big, florid-faced man hurried up to Longarm on the station platform. "Are you United States Deputy Marshal Custis Long?"

"That's right."

"I'm Marshal Pete Walker," the man said. "Let's walk back inside and take a seat where we can talk in private."

"Sure."

"He'd didn't do a damned thing!" the old man groused. "Just handed over his iron, his watch, and his wallet like everyone else. What kind of a federal marshal is he anyway!"

"An intelligent one," Walker snapped as he turned his back and stomped up into the empty coach where they could talk without being overheard.

As soon as they were seated, Walker came right to the point. "This is the third train robbery we've had up at Donner Pass in the last six months. From the passengers that I've already talked to, it sounds as if it's the same gang."

"Will they keep their word and let the women go?"

"I think so," Walker said. "At least they have in the past, although . . ."

"Although what?"

The marshal turned away with a sad shake of his head. "Well, they might be . . . violated."

Longarm's jaw muscles corded. "You mean this gang has *raped* its former hostages?"

"I'm afraid so." Walker's expression was bleak. "None of the women would admit it—you know, not wanting to be scandalized and all—but I could tell when we found them that they'd been violated. You could see that their lips were bruised and they were scratched up and in shock."

"Damn!" Longarm swore. "If I'd known that, I would have tried to do something to stop them."

"And gotten a whole lot of innocent people killed."

"Why haven't you been able to apprehend this gang?"

"They're smart and they travel light and fast. They never make a mistake and not one passenger or railroad employee has been able to recognize any of them."

"They've got to go somewhere after they rob the train."

"Sure they do, but where? I've worked with the authorities in Reno and our own state people in Sacramento. We've

13

had the best lawmen available, but they haven't been able to turn up a clue.''

"What about the women that were raped?'' Longarm asked. "Surely they must have been able to describe . . .''

"No,'' Walker said, "they couldn't . . . or wouldn't for fear of their lives.''

Longarm ground his teeth, then said, "I'd like to borrow a six-gun and a horse and ride up there to help you. I'm feeling damned rotten about letting those two women be taken.''

"Nothing else anyone could have done,'' Walker assured him. "At least no one was shot to death. That's the main thing.''

"Let's go,'' Longarm said impatiently.

"I thought I overheard someone say that you came here for that wedding between Stella Vacarro and Noah Huffington that takes place next Saturday.''

"That's right,'' Longarm said as he led the marshal back down the aisle so that they could get off the train and onto horses.

"Well,'' Walker told him, "if I were you, I wouldn't count on that wedding taking place.''

Longarm glanced back. "And why not?''

"I don't know. I've just got a feeling that it will be canceled for one reason or another. Mostly because of Mr. Abe Huffington. He's made no secret of how upset he is that his younger son is marrying a former whore and Comstock madam. He'll figure out some way to derail that marriage.''

Longarm decided he would have to develop a very thick skin until the wedding was over and he was on his way back to Denver. And if he couldn't do that, then he was just going to have to grit his teeth and endure the slander.

"This is Deputy Quaid," Walker said as soon as they jumped down on the platform. "Quaid, how many men could you round up on short notice for the posse?"

"I've got five men on good horses. They're all well armed and ready to go."

"This is Federal Deputy Marshal Custis Long from Denver. He's joining us."

Quaid was a slender six-footer with dark features. He wore rings on three of his fingers and a mustache very much like Longarm's. In his early twenties, Quaid had deep-set eyes with all the warmth of a reptile. Longarm's first impressions were usually pretty accurate, and he immediately judged Deputy Quaid as being a dandy and former gambler. The man wore a fine suit and tie and his boots glistened. His collar was starched, his hair stylishly long, and he had replaced the ordinary walnut handles on his Colt revolver with ivory.

"We got enough men now," Quaid said. "Don't need no federal lawmen mucking up things."

Longarm bristled. "I'm not going to 'muck up' anything," he snapped. "And there were at least five train robbers in that gang, probably another couple holding the horses in trees, and at least one to control the engineer and the train. You *definitely* need more men."

"He's right," Walker said. "And I damn sure don't want to hear any more about it from you, Deputy. Go get our horses and meet us at the office in five minutes."

Quaid spun on his heel and marched away as if he had a rod up his ass. Longarm shook his head. "He's a real warm and friendly fella, that one."

"No," Walker said, "he's a cold-blooded bastard, but he's good with a gun and fearless. People don't much like

Quaid and that's good, because I'll never have to worry about him trying to win my elective office.''

"I suppose that's one way to justify keeping someone like that. Where are the horses?''

"Let's go over to my office and I'll find you a spare six-gun. You might also want a rifle.''

"I sure would.''

The marshal's office was about what Longarm would have expected given the size of Auburn. It was modest, with two bunks in the lone cell, and two more bunks for the marshal and his deputy when they needed to spend the night guarding a prisoner or just wanted to take a little afternoon nap after a long, troublesome night. Other than the bunks and a couple of battered filing cabinets, there wasn't much else in the way of furniture except for a pair of old desks and worn office swivel chairs fit for the trash heap. The walls were covered with wanted posters, all yellow and flyspecked. Only the locked gun and rifle rack was clean and orderly.

"Here you go," Walker said, selecting a six-shooter and holster. "I took it off a hardcase only last week after he tried to rob a saloon and Quaid drilled him on the run.''

Longarm strapped on the holster and inspected the weapon. It was well used but in good working condition. "It will do fine," he said, wishing he had his own gun.

"That fella had a rifle too. It ain't pretty, but our gunsmith looked at it and said it was just fine.''

The Winchester was scarred but well oiled. A quick inspection left no doubts in Longarm's mind that the rifle and pistol were both accurate and dependable.

The marshal locked the door when they were outside, and turned to face a small and anxious crowd, many of them the very same first-class passengers that Longarm had already endured.

"All right, folks," Walker shouted over their excited chatter, "we're about to go after that gang of train robbers. We hope to pick up their trail and catch them either this evening or tomorrow."

"What makes you think so?" the banker yelled. "You haven't caught them yet and this is the third time they've struck in just the last six months!"

"Yeah, I know that, Mr. Haley, but they *have* to make a mistake sometime. Maybe this is the time. And, of course, our first responsibility will be to rescue those two young ladies even before we begin to worry about recovering any money or personal valuables."

Haley wasn't a bit satisfied with the marshal's promise, and he was still yelling and inciting the crowd when Quaid and their small posse arrived leading two saddled horses.

"Let's get out of here," Walker said to Longarm. "I sure hope that we can catch those sonsabitches. It's going to be hard to come back empty-handed again with the town elections only two months away."

Longarm took an instant dislike to the horse that Quaid had selected for him. It was a gangly, white-eyed, white-faced buckskin that snorted anxiously as Longarm lengthened the stirrups. It was clear that the animal was spooky and not to be trusted when it tried to take a hunk out of Longarm's backside.

"Mess with me," Longarm warned in a low, threatening voice, "and I'll shoot your damned big ears off!"

The buckskin laid its ears back flat against its head, but it didn't try to take a hunk out of him again.

"You about ready, for crissakes?" Quaid spat. "Marshal

Long, by the time you get in the saddle, those train robbers are likely to be in Idaho!''

Longarm ignored the caustic remark and mounted the buckskin, which immediately began to crow-hop around, trying to get its head low enough to really buck. Longarm lashed it with the ends of his reins and yanked its head up high so that the damned horse could not get any power in its bucking. The contest was over almost before it had begun. The buckskin, ears still laid back flat, allowed itself to be reined up the street, and then Longarm booted it with his heels and the big horse broke into a gallop along with the other horses.

It took nearly an hour to reach the site where the gang had left the train and taken to their waiting horses. Longarm went right to work studying tracks, and he could easily identify the smaller footprints of the young women hostages. He led the buckskin over to trees and yelled, ''All right, Marshal, here's where their trail begins! They're heading north!''

''They always do,'' Walker said, hurrying after him. ''And in the past, they've left their women hostages within a mile or two of where they took 'em.''

''Hope they didn't all screw 'em like that pretty girl they took off the last train they robbed,'' Quaid said with a wolf-ish grin that mocked his words.

The tracks were easy to follow as they snaked along a narrow trail up through the thick ponderosa pines. Out of respect for local authority, Longarm kept his horse back in line, but he wished he was in the lead for he was an excellent tracker. Walker's hastily formed posse was already struggling to keep up, and they were obviously a collection of local merchants. Longarm would rather have done without the inexperienced men because a mistake could get everyone ambushed and killed.

Two hours later, they entered a small mountain meadow and were startled to discover the two hostages. One of them was naked and in shock, sitting bent over in the grass and staring numbly at her bare legs. Her face had been battered and was already misshapen and discolored. The other young woman was half dressed, bloodied, and dazed.

"There they are!" Walker shouted, spurring his mount across the meadow.

When the posse came thundering into view, the half-dressed girl jumped up and started running.

"Hold up there!" Walker thundered. "I'm the marshal! We've come to help you!"

The girl was in her mid-twenties, short and a little chunky, with brown hair and wide, terror-stricken blue eyes. She stopped at Walker's voice and turned, her dress torn and hanging in shreds. It was clear that she had been raped, but that she'd put up a hard fight. Her cheeks were cut, one eye was swollen shut, and her lips were bleeding.

"Miss," Walker said, reining up his horse, "we're friends. We're going to help you."

The woman's hand fluttered to her mouth and then she screamed, "Where were you an hour ago when they were using us! When they beat and raped Sally almost to death!"

Her voice echoed off the mountains and Walker froze in his tracks. He bowed his head, removed his hat, and held it to his chest. "Miss, I'm real sorry but damned if we didn't come just as soon as we could."

"She *is* almost dead," one of the posse members said after removing his coat and covering the other woman. "This one needs a doctor."

19

"I wish *I* were dead!" the first woman cried.

Walker pulled off his heavy coat. "Why don't you put this on and let's get you both to a doctor."

"All right," the young woman agreed, her shoulders starting to heave as she succumbed to her grief.

Longarm rode a full circle around the meadow. He could see where the train robbers had angled to the east and that their trail was fresh. He trotted back to Walker. "I'm going after those men. Are you going with me?"

"You bet I am."

"I'll get the women back to Auburn and the doctor," Quaid offered.

"No!" The marshal lowered his voice. "Deputy, I need you to help us find and catch 'em."

Quaid couldn't seem to take his eyes off the two women. Watching him, Longarm thought he detected lust rather than compassion. Quaid, he decided, was a very dark and dangerous young man, one that the marshal didn't trust alone with the helpless, recently brutalized young women.

"Joe, you take care of these young women," Walker ordered an older man. "Double 'em up on your horse and lead them back to town. Keep 'em both covered. I don't want no gawkers, and we need to remember that these are *ladies*. Do you understand?"

"Sure do, Marshal."

"Good." Walker left the two young women to Joe's care and trod heavily back to his own horse. He appeared to Longarm to have aged considerably in just the last few minutes.

"Let's catch them murdering bastards!" Walker rasped. "And if we get them in our gun sights, I won't mind if someone accidentally pulls the trigger before they can surrender!''

Longarm felt the same way, but their sworn duty as lawmen was to apprehend even the worst criminals and take them to a court of law, not play God and execute them.

Chapter 3

Longarm was pretty sure that the train robbers were heading over the Sierra Nevada Mountains and planning to hide in Nevada. Since they were a smart, well-organized group, he expected that they might have a ranch or at least a hideout where they would lie low for a few weeks. It was fairly likely that they would also plot their next train or bank robbery, then drift into Reno or even back into California.

"We're going to lose 'em for sure if we don't overtake them by tomorrow," Deputy Quaid complained.

"Why do you say that?" Longarm asked.

"Hell, *you* ought to be able to figure out at least that much," Quaid growled. "Once they get on a main road, their tracks will be churned under by freight wagons and all manner of horse and mule traffic. I'll just bet anything that's going to happen. It's always happened before."

Longarm thought it was just about time to do a little educating. "Deputy Quaid, did you even bother to study the hoofprints in that meadow where we found those two young women?"

23

"Why . . . why sure!" Quaid blustered. "Of course I did."

"Then what can you tell me about them?"

"What do you mean?"

"I mean," Longarm said, his voice hardening, "did you notice *anything* out of the ordinary about *any* of their horses' hoofprints?"

Quaid squirmed in his saddle. "Well, one of them had thrown a shoe . . . I think."

"No," Longarm said, "but one of their horses did have a very distinctive bar across the back of its shoe. The kind a blacksmith puts on an animal when it needs corrective shoeing."

"Why, I know that!"

"Also, two of the outlaws were riding strawberry roans," Longarm continued. "I saw those horses when they mounted up and rode away from the train. That was a big mistake on their part. They should have kept their horses way back in the trees where they couldn't be seen. I expect they figured everyone they'd robbed would be too agitated to notice the color of their horses. Outlaws are often very taken, even vain about their horses . . . sort of like young men who have fancy guns and wax the tips of their mustaches."

Quaid's cheeks flushed red with anger. "Gawdammit, Marshal Long, I—"

"Save it!" Walker snapped. "Custis, what else did you notice about that gang?"

"Well," Longarm said, "they were all wearing masks, but the one that took my gun and watch had a very fine pair of dress boots. One of his pants legs had caught on the top of the boot, and I was able to notice that it was tooled with an eagle."

24

"So what are you going to do?" Quaid asked sarcastically, "go around pulling up pants legs?"

"No," Longarm replied, "but I'll recognize those boots when I see them again."

"Anything else?" Walker asked.

"A few small things," Longarm said, dismounting and gazing up through the trees. "Marshal Walker, have you ever chased this gang this far into the Sierras?"

"No. And why do you ask?"

"It would be easy to ambush us in this heavy timber, and they'd have all the advantage of surprise, superior numbers, and the high ground. I expect that at least a few of them are marksmen."

"They wouldn't bother with that!" Quaid scoffed. "Hell, by now they're ten or twenty miles away."

"If you feel so certain of that, then why don't *you* ride in the front?" Longarm offered.

Quaid was trapped. "Why, sure! I'm not afraid of any ambush."

"I'm the marshal," Walker said. "I should go first."

"No," Longarm told the man. "Let your deputy prove his point."

Quaid spurred his horse around them and took the lead. "If we catch them," he called back, "you had better believe I'll tell the folks back in Auburn who led this posse and who held back because they were so damned afraid!"

"Just follow their tracks," Longarm ordered. "You'll be able to pick that special bar-shoe out wherever the dirt is soft. Fortunately, its rider is a follower rather than a leader."

Deputy Quaid wasn't happy taking the lead, and the four remaining posse members were looking extremely nervous as they continued to follow the tracks along a river that wound through heavy stands of ponderosa pine.

Longarm rode behind Marshal Walker. His internal warning system was telling him that the train robbers were somewhere up ahead, probably watching their approach down the sights of their rifles. They'd been so cocky during their robbery that Longarm figured they were more than confident of their ability to wipe out a few unsuspecting posse members. They had good reason to be confident because they could empty two or three saddles in a single opening volley.

"Hold up!" Longarm called a few miles later as he reined his buckskin off the trail and into the cover of trees.

"What the hell is the matter now!" Quaid groused as he twisted around in his saddle.

"Quaid, do you see those high rocks about a hundred yards up the trail?"

"Sure, but . . ."

"They would give the gang we're following an excellent field of fire," Longarm said, dismounting and tying his horse behind some pine trees out of harm's way. "If I were an outlaw laying a trap, that's where I'd be hiding. You'll notice too that the forest widens away from the trail giving them enough time to unleash at least two or three shots at each of us before we could reach cover."

"You're just losing your damned nerve!" Quaid spat.

"No," Longarm said, "but I'm not about to offer myself up as an easy target."

"Damned if I'm scared!" Quaid spat, angrily spurring his horse up the trail.

"Quaid!" the marshal shouted. "Come back here!"

"He's got more nerve than good sense," Longarm said. "There's no stopping him now."

They watched as the deputy pushed his mount hard toward

the rocks. Two or three times Quaid glanced back, but he kept his horse going until he reached, then disappeared into the rocks.

"Well," one of the merchants who had joined the posse said, "I guess maybe Quaid just made us all look foolish."

"Maybe," Longarm said, still hearing that inner alarm in his head. "But I'm still going to leave my horse tied here and go ahead on foot."

"Now Marshal Long," Walker said, "I really don't think that's necessary."

"It is for me," Longarm replied. "And I suggest you and these good posse members just hunker down and wait right here until you see me up in those rocks waving that it's safe for you to come on ahead."

Walker looked at his small and inexperienced posse. A couple of them nodded to indicate that they much preferred to err on the side of caution.

"All right, Custis," Walker decided. "We'll give you fifteen minutes. No more. We can't keep doing this or we'll never overtake that gang."

"Agreed," Longarm said, dragging his rifle from its saddle boot, levering a fresh shell into its chamber, and then disappearing into the heavy forest.

Longarm was in good condition. Most men would have quickly been sucking for oxygen, but he was well accustomed to thin air because he lived in Denver. So Longarm worked his way up through the trees that flanked the trail Quaid had followed until he was almost to the jumble of broken rocks that formed a natural ambush.

Longarm practically stumbled into one of the train robbers. The outlaw had gone off a little ways to be alone, and now he was squatting down next to a pine tree, pants around his ankles as he took a dump on the pine needles. When he saw Longarm appear, he jumped up and tried to made a stab for his rifle leaning against the tree. Longarm swung the barrel of his own rifle in a tight arc that struck the outlaw just over his right ear. The man's eyes rolled up in his head and he collapsed.

Longarm hadn't meant to kill the outlaw, but that was exactly what had happened. He'd swung so hard that he'd crushed the train robber's skull. Removing a pistol from the dead man and jamming it into his coat, Longarm crept ahead, every nerve tingling. A few minutes later, he nearly stumbled over Deputy Quaid's body, which was lying facedown with a Bowie knife buried between his shoulder blades. The deputy's horse was gone, probably taken by the outlaws.

Longarm took a few moments to size up the opposition. How many ambushers had been left behind? That was the question. Maybe the whole gang was hidden in these rocks. Longarm figured that there was only one way to find out and that was to proceed with extreme caution.

It took him five minutes to circle around behind the ambushers. He counted just two more outlaws, both well hidden and with their rifles aimed down their back trail.

"I wonder what the hell happened to Milo," one of the ambushers complained, glancing off toward the trees. "He must have had the damned trots to take so long."

"He's always had gas and a sour stomach," the other ambusher replied. "Hell, Slim, I can smell Milo better'n a mile away."

"Are you sure you saw that posse way down below?" Slim asked, peering down the mountain.

"I think so. Least, I saw something moving up our back trail."

"Then it could have been a deer, a bear, or any other damned thing," Slim complained. "I don't much like waiting here while the boys push on ahead to the hideout."

"The boss said to wait until sundown in case we was followed. He said that there'd be whiskey to go with tonight's supper when we rode in late."

"Well, I know, but I sure wish Milo would get his ass back up here."

"He ain't worth spit anyway, so quit frettin' about him and keep your damned eyes peeled on our back trail."

Longarm preferred to watch and listen for a while in the hope that the two unsuspecting train robbers would mention the location of their hideout. But when the pair suddenly stiffened, Longarm knew that he'd run out of time.

"Here they come!" one of the ambushers whispered. "Five of them."

"Slim, you drill the first and third rider, I'll take the second and fourth. Then we'll both take care of the fifth. Make each shot count."

"It'll be like shooting fish in a barrel," Slim said, a wide grin creasing his brutish face.

Longarm raised his head. He saw Marshal Walker leading his pathetic little posse out of the trees. The marshal was also leading Longarm's mount, and it would only be a moment or two before the ambushers figured out that one of the posse must have scouted on ahead.

"Drop your rifles!" Longarm shouted, six-gun trained on the outlaws.

The pair of outlaws swung around and tried to fire their rifles. Longarm shot one in the chest and fired at Slim's legs in the hope of wounding the man rather than killing him outright.

"Ahhh!" Slim screamed, the rifle spilling from his hands as he took three slugs in his right leg and collapsed.

Longarm went over to remove the man's side arm, but he didn't need to hurry. Slim's knee had been shattered beyond recognition by one big .44-caliber slug and Longarm's other two bullets had riddled the outlaw's thigh. Unfortunately, at least one of the slugs had severed a major artery and the man was bleeding profusely.

"You sonofabitch!" Slim cried. "I'm bleeding to death!"

Longarm untied the man's bandanna, probably the same one that Slim had worn when he'd robbed the train. He twirled it around a few times and then tied it around the man's leg above the wound to serve as a tourniquet. The bleeding slowed, but it wouldn't stop.

"Slim, you're finished," Longarm grimly pronounced. "Why don't you die with a clear conscience and tell me where the rest of your gang went."

"Go to Hell!"

"You're liable to go straight to Hell if you don't do the right thing," Longarm told the ashen-faced outlaw. "Where is your hideout?"

"Damned if I'll tell you!"

"And that's your final word?"

"Hell, yes!"

"Too bad," Longarm said. "But I guess we'll find them anyway. Can't be far if they were holding supper for you. Maybe I'll eat it instead."

Slim's lips pulled back to reveal rotting teeth. His face was dirty and unshaven, filled more with hate than fear. "You sonofabitch!" he choked. "You'll never . . ."

But whatever last words he had were lost when Slim was seized by a sudden and violent convulsion. Longarm heard the man's death rattle, and then saw his body relax as he expelled his final breath.

Ten minutes later, Marshal Walker and his badly spooked posse reached the rocks to gape at the dead outlaws.

"You killed all three of them?"

"I meant to take at least one of them alive," Longarm admitted. "But I did overhear this pair say that they had a supper waiting at the outlaws' hideout. That means that the rest can't be too far ahead."

"I'm all for going back to Auburn!" one of the posse members exclaimed. "We've already done more than our share and now we've lost Deputy Quaid. Dammit, I don't want to be the next one to take a bullet."

Then another man spoke up. "I got a wife and two kids. We need more men if we're going to try and jump the rest of that gang. I say we ride back to Auburn and get some more volunteers."

"No," Walker said gruffly. "By the time we return, the outlaws will have cleared out. We *know* that they're waiting supper tonight. I say we take our chances and finish them off while we have the element of surprise."

"I couldn't agree more," Longarm said.

"Well I *disagree*," the first posse member railed. "I'll take Quaid's body back to town and try to get you some help, but this is as far as I'm riding."

"Me too," a third added. The others nodded in agreement.

"Then I guess it's just you and me," Longarm said to Walker.

"Yep," Walker replied, staring at Quaid's body. "We have to finish this."

"Marshal Walker," one of the posse members wheedled, "I sure do wish you'd change your mind. We could be back

31

here with more men by this time tomorrow. Can't you just wait that long?''

''No,'' Walker said, ''we can't. I keep seeing those young women's battered faces and remembering the others that were raped and beaten. And there's also Deputy Quaid. So you boys lay him across a horse and take him and these others back for burying. Me and Custis will push on and do whatever it takes to bring the rest of those outlaws to rope justice.''

''Marshal Walker,'' Longarm said while grimly reloading his pistol, ''I couldn't agree with you more.''

Chapter 4

Longarm selected the best of the outlaws' horses and ordered the four frightened posse members to return his ill-natured buckskin along with the bodies to Auburn.

"We'd sure like to come along with you and finish off those bastards," one of the posse members swore as they were preparing to leave. "It's just that—"

"Never mind," Walker told the nervous merchant. "You volunteered and you've done yourself and our town a service. Nothing more is expected—or needed."

"But you'll be outnumbered! Marshal Walker, why don't you just give us one day and—"

"So long, Jim," Walker said. "When the folks in town ask, you tell them that Federal Marshal Long are I are finally going to put an end to this gang."

"Sure thing," Jim said, shaking Walker's and then Longarm's hand. "You don't have a family, do you, Marshal Long?"

"No."

"Well, if you did—"

"Thanks," Longarm interrupted. "And we all need to get moving before we run out of daylight."

"Yeah," Jim said, mounting his horse. "So long!"

Neither Longarm nor Marshal Walker waited around to watch the posse members ride back down the mountain toward Auburn. They needed to find the outlaws' hideout before darkness closed in on them or the gang members began to go their separate ways.

Longarm took the lead. Fortunately, the bar-shoe track was still among those continuing deeper into the mountains. And because there had been a lot of rain and snow during the winter, the ground was soft and the tracks easy to follow.

"Are there any lakes in these parts?" Longarm asked, twisting around to look back at Walker.

"There's one or two, I believe. Used to be a lot of old gold camps up here too. All of 'em abandoned by the early 1860s after the last of the placer gold petered out and everyone rushed over to the Comstock Lode to strike it rich."

"Were you ever a prospector?"

"Oh, sure," Walker said. "I came here with all the other fools during the Forty-Niner gold rush. It was one hell of a stampede, I'll tell you. I arrived on a sailing ship from Boston that almost sank off Cape Horn. Got here in the fall of 1850, but all the best claims were already taken along the American, Bear, and Rubicon Rivers. Even so, I had my chances to be rich. Struck a few glory holes, but I pissed it all away on women and the gambling tables. Only vice I never had was a love of liquor. Always made me sicker than a dog. But I loved those pretty girls that come to the gold camps!"

"So how did you wind up a lawman in Auburn?"

"I was getting too old to prospect and caught pneumonia

34

in the winter of '55. A lot of men died of it. Panning gold in those cold rivers and streams quickly took its toll on your joints. I was still young back then, but already creaking around like an old man. I started looking for healthier things to do.''

"And you chose to be a lawman."

"Seemed logical. I was always a pretty fair hand with a pistol, and when a gunman named Red Beamon shot up the town, I went out and tried to get him to drop his weapons. He wouldn't, so we started shooting at each other right in the middle of the street. He was drunk, I was sober, and I'm sure you can figure the outcome.''

"Did you kill him?"

"Damn right! I shot him deader than a skunk because I knew, when he sobered up and posted bail, he would come gunning for me and probably have the edge. He was faster."

"But you were steadier and smarter," Longarm said, drawing his horse up so that Walker could ride alongside. "I was also wondering why a veteran like you ever hired a fool like Deputy Quaid."

Walker smiled thinly. "You didn't have much use for him, did you."

"No. He was arrogant and hotheaded. A kid like that has no business putting on a badge. I can't imagine why you hired him in the first place."

"Actually, he was my sister's illegitimate son. When she died a few years ago, she asked me to take care of Mark. Try to straighten him out. So I taught him how to handle a gun, but when he got good at it he became . . . well, it just went to his damned head."

"You didn't shed any tears when you saw his body."

"He was bound to get killed," Walker said. "The only

question I ever had was if he'd take a few with him.''

"He didn't," Longarm said. "He just charged into those rocks and one of the outlaws put a knife into his back and that was the end of him.''

Walker heaved a deep sigh. "I'm just glad that my sister died before her son. Mark was always a problem, and I figured it was because he had no father. I tried to be his father, but that never worked. Mark was always angry, mostly at himself.''

Longarm nodded with understanding for he'd known a lot of men who had died young and angry. They were most all driven by a fierce need to prove themselves braver and tougher than anyone else. Sometimes they just got into a lot of fistfights until someone stomped the living hell out of them and they either wised up or got hurt so badly they couldn't ever fight again. Either way, they usually ended up bitter and broken. It was a rare one indeed that shaped up to become a good, hardworking citizen.

"You been a United States marshal for a long time?" Pete Walker asked.

"Quite a while.''

"Well," Walker said, "you're in charge now. I'm past my prime and I don't often do this kind of thing. So you just tell me what to do and it'll work better that way.''

"Thanks," Longarm said. "It's a wise man who knows his limitations.''

"You killed three men up in those rocks. That's more men than I've killed in all the years that I've been Auburn's only town marshal. That tells me that you're a better man at this sort of thing than I am.''

Longarm came to an opening in the trees, and then he

36

whirled his horse around and drove it back into cover with Walker close behind.

"You saw them?"

"I saw a ghost town with some visitors," Longarm replied as he tied his horse and yanked his rifle from its saddle boot.

"Well, how do you know it isn't just some cowboys or travelers passing through?"

"I recognized a pair of strawberry roans," Longarm answered. "They're not the kind you forget once you've laid eyes on them. These are definitely our train robbers, rapists, and murderers, Pete."

After tying their horses where they would not be seen, Longarm and Walker crept back to the edge of the forest and flattened on the pine needles to study the old mining town.

"You ever been here before?" Longarm asked.

"Nope."

"Well," Longarm said, "it looks about like every other mining town that I've ever seen that went boom and then bust. Just a few main stores falling down because they weren't ever built to last more than a couple of years. Some old mining equipment scattered along that streambed, and that's it."

"I expect that you'll want to wait for dark before we go in after them?"

"Be a good idea," Longarm replied. "But we have to remember that they're expecting Slim and them other two to show up pretty soon."

"I forgot about that."

Longarm scrubbed his jaw. "Pete, I'm thinking maybe we can just ride in after dark and they'll mistake us for the pair I shot back in the rocks."

"But what if they don't?"

"Then we have ourselves a shooting match, only we'll be sober and they'll have been celebrating and be at least half drunk." Longarm glanced sideways at the older man. "Do you have any better ideas?"

"Can't say as I do."

"Then let's sit tight until it gets good and dark before we ride in."

"How many do you think are left?"

"I count seven horses in the street there, so that's what I'm figuring on," Longarm said. "Can you hear the music?"

"Yep. A fiddle and a guitar."

Longarm stretched out and gazed up at the sky. "I wonder if they've got women."

"Wouldn't surprise me," Walker said. "Do you know how much money was on that train they just robbed?"

"No."

"In addition to what they took from the passengers, just over fifteen thousand dollars. A full month's payroll for one of our biggest local mining companies. And if I don't recover it, a hell of a lot of hardworking Auburn families are going to suffer. The loss could put the Sierra Mining Company out of business."

"We'll get the payroll back," Longarm promised. "They couldn't have had the time to spend it yet."

"That's another reason that I knew we couldn't wait to get this gang," Walker said. "Once these boys hit the big towns like Sacramento, Reno, or even San Francisco, we can kiss that mining payroll good-bye."

"Why don't we take a little nap so that we'll be fresh when we go in tonight," Longarm suggested.

Walker chuckled. "You're sure a cool one. I'm afraid to

38

take a nap. At my age, I might not wake up until tomorrow morning.''

"Don't worry," Longarm told him. "I'll wake you up a couple of hours after dark."

"Well, in that case," Walker said, removing his hat and stretching out full length on a soft bed of pine needles, "why not?"

When Longarm awoke, he peered up through the pines and figured it was a little before midnight. They'd slept a good six hours, and he knew the outlaws would have been drinking and carousing during all that time. It would give him and Walker a crucial edge.

"Time to wake up, Pete," he said, nudging the lawman.

Walker sat up, scrubbed his eyes, and yawned. "I was dreaming that I was home in bed instead of out here in the forest waiting to go in and shoot it out with those train robbers."

"Maybe we won't have to do all that much shooting," Longarm told the man. "Maybe we can get the drop on most of them and get the rest to surrender."

"Not much chance of that," Walker pointed out, "considering that they've raped and murdered. There's no question in anyone's mind that they'll hang."

"I see your point," Longarm said, nodding in agreement.

They both went to their horses, tightened their cinches, and prepared to ride into the town. If anything the music and laughter had grown louder through the evening, and that was fine with Longarm. He wanted the outlaws to be drunk and sloppy.

"Don't you think that they'll at least have guards posted?"

"I doubt it. These boys have pulled a lot of holdups and never had a problem before tonight."

"We're not going to just ride into the middle of town, tie these horses in front of the saloon, and waltz inside telling them they are under arrest—are we?"

"Nope," Longarm said as they entered the main street lined with weeds and collapsing rock and wood buildings. "They may be drunk, but they still outnumber us almost four to one. What we had better do is . . ."

Longarm's words died on his lips as one of the outlaws and a woman emerged onto the street from between a pair of buildings. The man's shirt was unbuttoned and so were his pants. The woman was disheveled and trying to drag the top of her dress over her enormous bare breasts. They were sharing a bottle of whiskey. Longarm saw the amber glint of liquor in moonlight as the woman flipped the bottle up and drank like a big, thirsty horse. The man buried his face between her breasts, and they tripped and fell down laughing.

"Come on, Ginny," he bellowed, "this time I'm going to screw you right in the middle of this street."

Ginny took another big pull on the bottle, then rolled over onto her back and hauled up her dress. The outlaw got his pants down around his knees and mounted the big woman. Longarm watched them rut like a couple of fat hogs, and then he dismounted and quietly handed his reins to Walker. Removing his gun, he circled around behind and pistol-whipped the humping outlaw across the back of his head. The man groaned and collapsed. Ginny, thinking he was finished, rolled him off and took another drink. That was when she finally noticed Walker and Longarm.

"Who the hell are you?" she asked, fat legs still spread wide.

Longarm said nothing.

"He's finished," she announced, "so you boys got anything for me to drink?"

"No."

"Then it'll cost you each a dollar to climb on," she said, giving them a coarse, lopsided grin. "But you better hurry while it's still hot."

Longarm shook his head. "How many more of them, Ginny?"

"What do you mean?"

"How many more outlaws and women?"

"Who cares? I got everything you boys need!"

Longarm dragged the outlaw aside. He rolled Ginny over on her belly. She didn't seem offended. In fact she laughed, then said, "If you boys like me better from behind, just make sure you poke the right hole!"

Longarm turned around and Walker threw him a rope. He quickly bound Ginny's hands behind her back and then hog-tied her. Ginny squirmed. "This way is going to cost you extra, big boy!"

He stuffed his bandanna into her mouth, and that was when Ginny finally got upset enough to start thrashing.

Longarm didn't care. "Pete," he called, "tie the horses up behind this building and come help me drag this pair inside where no one will stumble across them until we've taken care of the rest."

"Sure enough," Walker said, quickly dismounting.

Ginny must have weighed three hundred pounds, and they had a hell of a time dragging her over the front doorstep and into the ruined old building. She was fighting and cussing and squalling, but she couldn't spit out the gag because Longarm had jammed it too far down her throat.

41

Longarm removed the unconscious outlaw's coat and hat, then exchanged them for his own.

"One down and six to go," he said as they left the pair and went back to the street.

"Looks like most of the commotion is coming from that big two-storied building," Walker remarked.

"I expect that you're right. Saloon downstairs, rooms upstairs."

"That would be my guess," Walker said. "What are we going to do now?"

"We'll just take our time," Longarm replied. "We've got all night to even the odds."

"Damn near busted my back helping you carry that big woman."

"Me too," Longarm said, studying the saloon.

"What—"

"Hey, Slim! That you?"

"Uh-oh," Walker breathed. "Here comes another loving couple."

"Just let me handle them."

"After what I've seen so far, I wouldn't dream of interfering, Custis."

Longarm walked across the street with his hat pulled down low over his face. Fortunately, there was only a crescent moon and the light was poor. "Yeah," he answered, "it's Slim."

"Hey," the outlaw called, hugging his woman tight. "Lola here needs a fresh man with some fresh spending money. She's about broke me."

"Only cost you three dollars," Lola said to Longarm, cocking her hips and batting her long eyelashes.

Even in the semi-darkness Longarm could see that Lola

was young, slender, and seductive. He judged her to be no more than twenty-five, and she smelled like rose water.

"Sounds good to me," Longarm said, taking three quick steps and then unleashing a wicked uppercut that originated at his boot top and ended at the point of the outlaw's chin. The man was lifted completely off the ground and knocked out cold. Longarm bent over and removed his six-gun.

"Why did you do that to your friend?" Lola asked with surprise.

"Well, I never really considered him a friend," Longarm answered. "Pete, why don't you take Lola for a walk."

"Me?"

"Why, sure!" Lola said, delighted.

"I think you can handle it," Longarm told him.

Pete gulped. "I don't know," he said, "but I'd sure like to give it a helluva try!"

Lola peered closely at Walker. "It will cost you five dollars."

"But you told my friend it'd only cost him *three* dollars!"

"You're older and slower," Lola said, taking Walker's arm. "But I like men who take their time and have a little age on them."

Walker grinned like a loon. He winked at Longarm and said, "What about . . ."

Longarm started toward the saloon. "I'm just going to have a look-see," he called back.

He boldly walked right up to the front door of the old saloon and peeked inside. The place had once been quite a gambling hall, but all the chandeliers had long ago been shot to pieces. There were some bullet-riddled paintings on the walls, and a lot of cobwebs in the open rafters. But mostly, Longarm was assessing the outlaws and liking what he saw.

43

The remaining gang members were having a high old time. One of them was playing a guitar, one a fiddle, and two others were drunkenly prancing about with a pair of gals that that made Lola look better than ever. A fifth outlaw sat alone at a table with a whiskey bottle.

Longarm eased back outside and sat down on the broken boardwalk. He drew a cheroot from his vest pocket, and was reminded that one of these men still had his Ingersoll watch and chain. Longarm thought he knew which one too. When he lit his cheroot, he inhaled deeply and examined the six-gun he'd taken off the last outlaw. As expected, it was loaded and in good working condition. Longarm figured that, sooner or later, at least a few of the outlaws would tromp outside for a breath of fresh air. And when they did, he'd even the odds without having to kill anyone.

Within ten minutes, one of the train robbers did sway drunkenly through the doorway. He didn't notice Longarm until it was much too late, and by then, his eyes were rolled up in his head and his chin was resting in the dirt.

"Three down, four to go," Longarm told himself after dragging the unconscious man out of sight and returning to the front door of the saloon to finish his smoke.

Almost half an hour passed before Pete Walker emerged from across the street.

"You sound winded to me," Longarm said, teasing the older man, who looked pretty disheveled.

"That Lola is a tiger!"

"What did you do with her?"

"Do you have to ask a question like that?"

"No, I mean after you laid her."

"Oh. Well, the first thing I did was to show her my badge and tell her we were both lawmen here to arrest those mur-

44

dering thieves. She said the women have horses outside of town, and I gave her a chance to get away clean.''

''You're a pretty trusting fellow,'' Longarm said, not sure that he approved. ''What if Lola the Tiger decides to warn those boys inside?''

''She won't,'' Walker assured him. ''I gave her an extra twenty dollars. I asked her to come visit me in Auburn and promised that she'd have no trouble in my town.''

Longarm tossed the butt of his cheroot into the street. ''Pete, let's march right into that saloon and end it right now.''

''All right,'' Walker said, drawing his gun. ''Might as well get it over with.''

Longarm had a gun in each fist when he barged inside. ''Freeze!'' he yelled. ''You're all under arrest!''

Two of the outlaws took a strong and fatal objection to Longarm's order, and he gunned them both down as they drunkenly fumbled for their side arms. The other pair attempted to make a wild dash out the back door, but Pete shot one in the leg and the other tripped and fell heavily, making it easy for Longarm to pounce on his back.

''Hold still or I'll put you to sleep permanently,'' Longarm warned.

The man froze. Then Longarm saw his .44-.40 Colt in the man's holster.

''You're the one with the fancy boots,'' Longarm said, dragging the outlaw to his feet. ''And you're also the one that robbed me on the train and took my gun and pocket watch and gold chain.''

''What are you talking about!''

Longarm retrieved his weapon, then searched the man and quickly found his missing watch. ''This,'' he growled, spinning the fellow around and propelling him toward the marshal. "Handcuff him, Pete!"

Longarm went to see if he could save the wounded man from bleeding to death. As it turned out, the fellow had only suffered a flesh wound.

"Another two inches higher and you'd be a singing like a soprano," he told the outlaw.

"What about us!" one of the whores cried.

"You can go back to whatever cave you crawled out of," Longarm told them. "You're lucky that we don't arrest you."

"For what!"

"Spending stolen money," Walker growled.

The girls tromped out knowing the party was over, but not before Walker searched and relieved them of their stolen money. A short time later, Longarm discovered three saddlebags full of money and jewelry hidden upstairs. He and Walker put it all together and the money added up to nearly twenty-five thousand dollars.

"I'll bet some of the girls are holding out a few dollars on us," Longarm said.

"If it's Lola, I'll be happy to frisk her, but if it's Ginny, well, she can keep the money because I'm not touching her again."

"My sentiments exactly," Longarm agreed. "Any idea how soon these men will be in court after we haul them into Auburn?"

"They'll be tried next week and hanged the very next day," Walker assured him.

"Good," Longarm said. "Justice is best when it's swift."

Chapter 5

Longarm twisted around in his saddle to regard his friend as they approached Auburn. "Marshal Walker?"

"Yeah?"

"Let's trade places," Longarm said, reining his horse aside. "This is your town so you ought to ride in front. I'll take the rear."

Walker smiled with gratitude. "You're a hell of a fine fellow, know that?"

"Not really. What I *do* know is that you're a credit to our profession and deserve to be re-elected as Auburn's town marshal. This won't hurt your chances any."

"That's for sure," Walker said, trotting up in front and leading their five prisoners into town.

The reaction was just about what Longarm had expected. People came pouring out of the shops and saloons, and when they saw Walker leading the badly whipped train robbers, along with two of their dead companions, folks of all ages began to applaud, then cheer. Walker blushed with pride and tipped his hat while trying to look stern and official. It tickled Longarm to see the older man get the credit. He had grown to like and respect Walker, and was pretty sure that this day would not soon be forgotten in this bustling Sierra gold rush town.

When they arrived at the marshal's office, Walker roughly ordered his prisoners to dismount and, still making a good show of it, marched them into his jail cell at the point of his six-gun.

"Marshal Walker! This town owes you a tremendous debt," a nattily dressed man in a gray suit loudly proclaimed.

"Well, Mayor, I appreciate that, but I have to give a lot of the credit to United States Deputy Marshal Custis Long— and to my brave posse and slain deputy. God rest Mark Quaid's poor soul."

"Yes," the mayor replied, suddenly looking quite grave. "We received his poor body and that of the other dead outlaws. The undertaker hasn't had so much business in a long, long time."

"Let's just hope that it's a long time before he does again," Walker said, locking his crestfallen prisoners in the cell and turning to regard the admiring crowd.

"Is this the same bunch that has robbed all the other trains coming over Donner Pass?" an eager reporter with a pad and pencil asked.

"There is no question about that," Walker told the reporter. "We recovered almost all of the loot from this last holdup as well as the passengers' jewelry. I'm sure that there is also some jewelry that we can tie to the earlier robberies. Wouldn't you expect so, Marshal Long?"

"Definitely."

"So how did you track them all the way to their hiding place?" the reporter asked, pencil poised over writing pad.

Walker looked to Custis for the answer, but he just

shrugged. "Well," Walker began, "you see, Marshal Long had seen that two of the train robbers were riding roan horses, but the *really* important key was in identifying a particular horseshoe that made following their tracks fairly easy—if a man is an *expert* tracker, that is."

"You're a credit to our fine city, Marshal Walker, and you'll certainly have my support for re-election."

"Well thank you very much, Mayor Yarrow! Does that mean that the city council will finally approve my long-overdue twenty-five-dollar-a-month raise?"

The mayor was caught off guard. Longarm was highly amused as everyone just stood there, waiting for Mayor Yarrow's answer. He had no choice but to agree.

"It'll be reflected in your next paycheck, Marshal Walker. You have my word on it."

"That's good enough for me," Walker said, slapping the smaller man on the back hard enough to drive him two steps forward. "But right now, Marshal Long and I need to question my surviving prisoners and find out if we can recover any more stolen cash or jewelry."

"Why would they agree to help you do that?" the reporter asked. "Seeing as how everyone knows they'll hang anyway."

"We can't say that for sure," Walker objected. "These men deserve a fair trial. We'll let a judge and a jury decide their fate."

"They ought to have their balls shot off!" one of the townspeople cried loudly. As if to emphasize his point, he yanked his six-gun out of his holster and fired a bullet into the ceiling, showering everyone with plaster. "And I'm plenty ready to do it!"

Longarm jumped forward and grabbed the weapon, then

wrenched it from the man's grasp. "Get out of here!" he ordered, shoving him back out the doorway. "Are you trying to get someone else killed?"

"Just them prisoners! We don't need a judge or jury! I say we string them up right now!"

The crowd was all for the idea, and Longarm could see that Walker needed to take control or else the townspeople really would turn into a lynch mob.

To his credit, Walker drew his own gun and fired it into the ceiling causing another shower of plaster. "All right, everyone!" he bellowed. "Out of my office! They'll be no lynching in Auburn—not as long as I'm your marshal who has sworn to faithfully uphold the law!"

"You're right, Marshal," the mayor said, backing out with the rest of them, "but we *are* running over our budget and a trial *is* expensive, not to mention feeding five prisoners until they are hanged. And what with your new *raise,* we could use some savings here."

"Not a chance," Walker growled. "You find a legal way to cut expenses and it better not be my raise!"

"Of course not," the mayor said. "However . . ."

"Find a judge and ask him to set a trial *this* week. It shouldn't take more than an hour to select a jury, hear the evidence, and reach a verdict—well, two hours at the most."

Longarm helped to usher the crowd back outside. He slammed the door shut and turned to face Walker. "It looks to me like we could have some problems tonight."

"I doubt that."

"Let's hope not," Longarm said. "But just in case, I'd be happy to bunk here and . . ."

"No, no," Walker said quickly. "Custis, you've already done more than enough. And though I didn't tell the townspeople, you and I both know that I couldn't have brought these five outlaws in without your help.''

''Everyone needs help sometimes.''

''Yes,'' Walker agreed, ''but you came here for a wedding and vacation, and so far, it hasn't been much fun. Why don't you go and see Miss Vacarro? She lives in that big Victorian with the green shutters on High Street. You can't miss it.''

''I guess there's some . . . controversy about that wedding?''

''That's putting it mildly. Young Noah Huffington, as I'm sure you've heard, was a minister and he was engaged to a very popular and outstanding young lady. The whole town approved of that wedding, and they hold Miss Vacarro entirely to blame for it being called off.''

''Why was it called off?''

''No one really knows,'' the marshal replied. ''Who can explain matters of the heart? Obviously, Noah Huffington— despite his family's strong objections—fell *out* of love with his former fiancée and fell *in* love with Miss Vacarro. And maybe they'll make a wonderful couple and live happily ever after.''

''I can tell from the sound of your voice that you think that is extremely unlikely.''

''You're right. The town was shocked. Abe Huffington's career is now in jeopardy, and everyone has their own pet theory as to why Noah dumped Miss Carole Clark and asked Stella to be his wife. Most people believe that the young minister is being blackmailed.''

''Blackmailed?''

''That's right. You see, the Huffington family is very, very wealthy and powerful. And before Noah became a Christian, he was known to be a little wild and not adverse to sewing

51

his oats in many fertile fields—if you catch my drift.''

"I do.''

"Well, then,'' Walker said, "most people think that he might even have fathered an illegitimate child.''

"Stella's child?''

Walker shrugged. "She left Auburn for several months. When she came back, she looked unwell. The most popular rumor is that she had a baby and gave it away for adoption. But that she is using the child to blackmail her way into the Huffington fortune.''

Longarm snorted with disgust. "That's ridiculous! Stella might be guilty of many things, but she has far too much pride to do something *that* low-down.''

"Who knows? If she lands Noah Huffington, that puts her in line for the family wealth. Old Abe swears that he will write Noah out of his will if he marries Stella, but I know that he won't.''

"Why not?''

"Because his wife died several years ago and the couple only had two children. Noah and his older brother, Nick. Nick has always tried to follow in his father's footsteps, but he is mean and drinks way too damn much. He gets drunk, gambles badly, and loses all his money, then gets into vicious fights. He's a bad one, and I've had nothing but trouble with him for years. Nick Huffington is everything that you *wouldn't* want your own son to be.''

"The exact opposite of Noah.''

"Yes,'' the marshal said with a shake of his head. "I can't explain why one turned out so damned rotten and the other so good, but that's the way it happened.''

"I see. Does this Nick also live in Auburn?''

"You could say that,'' Walker replied. "He sort of hangs

around the western Sierra gold camps. He might show up drunk in Coloma one week, then in Sonora, and then wear out his welcome and ride up to raise hell in Nevada City. He's big trouble, and almost always hangs out with a couple of hardcases just as bad as he himself.''

"Why doesn't his father disown him?''

"Abe has thought about it. If you ask me, Nick is the one who is really into the blackmailing business. He walks the line of the law just enough to keep himself from going to prison and really embarrassing his father or ruining his political future. Abe can't stand Nick, and although he is bitterly disappointed in Noah's decision to marry Miss Vacarro, he likes Noah far better than Nick. The truth is, you can't help but like and admire Noah.''

"I see," Longarm said, not sure that he really did see the whole picture. "Well, I came here to attend a wedding and that's what I'm going to do. So I'll just leave all that other stuff alone.''

"Be the best idea," Walker said in agreement. "The wedding is to take place next Saturday afternoon at the Grange Hall.''

"I thought it was to be a church wedding.''

"It was," Walker admitted, "but every church in town declined to let it take place.''

"But why?''

"Because their pastors were afraid of angering their church membership and losing out at the donation plate.''

"That figures," Longarm said. "What did they have to do, *import* a more tolerant minister?''

"That's right. One from Sacramento who doesn't have to worry about antagonizing his parishioners.''

Longarm shook his head, then strolled back to the crowded

jail cell and regarded the five men. To the one with the bullet wound, he said, "I'm sure that there will be a doctor to look at that wound."

"You big sonofabitch!" the outlaw snarled. "Who cares about a scratch if I'm going to hang anyway!"

"Good point."

"We ever get out of this mess," another of the outlaws warned, "you're a dead man."

"You *won't* get out of this alive," Longarm promised as he turned and walked away.

When he emerged from the marshal's office, there was still a large crowd milling around outside. Longarm studied them for a moment, wondering if he should just stay out of this trouble. But then, he decided that he ought to make his own position clear.

"I understand why you people are angry and eager to see those train robbers swing," he began, "but it *has* to be done according to the law. Necktie justice is a step backward."

A huge, full-bearded miner who reeked of rotgut whiskey shoved his way forward. He was as tall as Longarm and a good twenty pounds heavier. When he spoke, the whiskey fumes on his breath were potent enough to kill flies.

"Marshal, we appreciate what you did to help out, but the best thing you could do now would be to get back on that train and get the hell out of Auburn. This isn't none of your damned business anymore."

"You're dead wrong about that," Longarm told the man. "I'm a federal marshal and I'm sworn to uphold the law. And that's why, if you are getting any funny ideas about taking the law into your own hands, you're going to have to get past me as well as Marshal Walker."

"Oh," the huge miner said, "I don't expect that would be much of a problem."

"Try me and find out," Longarm said, hands balling at his sides.

"And get arrested for beating hell out of a federal officer? No, thanks! You just take your little tin badge, get on the big train, and keep going."

Longarm smiled thinly. "I'll tell you this just one time. Turn around and leave, mister. And while you're at it, take everyone else with you."

"Bert, you gonna let him talk to you that way?" another miner challenged.

Bert laughed even as he drove his knee upward, intent on crushing Longarm's testicles. But the man was slow and unsteady because of his drinking, so Longarm had no trouble turning sideways and deflecting the attack. At the same time, he slammed his fist into Bert's solar plexus, and followed that with a left cross that sent him reeling.

The crowd caught Bert and held him on his feet until he could focus again. Then, they shoved him back at Longarm. Bert charged swinging from all angles, and Longarm ducked three punches but took a wild overhand to the side of the head that rocked him to his foundations and put stars in his eyes.

"Get him, Bert! Get him!" some of the miners shouted.

Bert snorted like a bull and tried to grab Longarm and crush him. Ducking and retreating, Longarm bought a few precious minutes by managing to elude the miner's charges. But the bells were still ringing in his head when Bert aimed another kick at his groin. Longarm managed to grab the miner's boot with both hands and heave it upward. Bert slammed down on his back so hard that the wind gushed from his lungs. Longarm didn't wait for him to recover. He dropped on the man's chest and sledged him four or five times in the face, breaking Bert's nose and opening a wicked gash across his cheek.

"He's had enough!" someone cried.

Longarm climbed off the bloodied and dazed miner. He shook the cobwebs out of his own head and then said, "I'll tell you just one more time—disperse!"

The miners, angry and disappointed, dragged Bert to his feet and over into a saloon. Longarm touched the side of his face and felt the swelling. He turned to see Marshal Walker standing in the doorway with a shotgun in his hands.

"Who were you going to use that scattergun on?" Longarm asked the town marshal. "Them or me?"

Walker chuckled. "Seeing as how they have a vote in Auburn and you don't, Marshal Long, I reckon you can figure that one out for yourself."

Longarm knew that the lawman was teasing. Flexing his hands and then rubbing his stinging knuckles, he shook his head and headed on down the street a few steps before he turned and looked back. "Walker?"

"Yeah?"

"If you have trouble tonight, I'll come running."

"I'm in good shape," Walker said. "The trouble is over now, thanks to your help."

"I hope you're right," Longarm said. "By the way, where can I find High Street?"

"You're going in the right direction. Two blocks south, then turn right. And give my best regards to Miss Vacarro."

"That surprises me."

"Why?"

"Well, I just didn't have the impression that you thought much of Stella."

"Oh, that's not true," Walker said. "Stella has always played it square with me. I've never had a minute worth of trouble from her or her saloon. She's a hell of a good businesswoman and runs an honest house."

"That doesn't surprise me," Longarm said, turning and walking down the street.

Chapter 6

Longarm had passed through Auburn on the train going to Sacramento a time or two, but he'd never really had a good look at the old mining town. Now, as he headed off to find Stella, he could see that Auburn had enjoyed quite a bit of prosperity in its heyday before the rich ore deposits had finally begun to peter out. The old section of town had apparently been razed by a fire and rebuilt, so that it now had the look of permanence with an impressive firehouse, a big Masonic hall, and the Wells Fargo office. The Union Bar was doing a good business, and Longarm could hear organ music and a choir practicing in the Pioneer Methodist Church.

The city's broad streets were lined with trees, and most of the houses were constructed of either rock or brick and had lawns and gardens. It was a handsome town, one of the few that had obviously been blessed by the arrival of the railroad. There was little doubt that Auburn had a bright and lasting future.

Longarm had no trouble finding High Street, and he was not surprised to see that it was in one of nicest parts of the town. Stella Vacarro had always sought respectability, and it would be like her to buy a proper Victorian house just like any other successful business owner.

When he came to Stella's place, Longarm leaned on a white picket fence and studied the house with its blooming red roses. It was an ideal home, and only needed a few children playing tag in the yard to fit the dream of what most working-class Americans hoped to one day achieve.

Longarm opened the gate and climbed the wide porch, then knocked on the front door. Stella appeared looking as pretty as ever, despite dark circles under her eyes.

"Custis!" she cried, knocking open the screen door and throwing herself into his arms. "I was wondering if you'd make it before or after my wedding!"

"Well," he said a little sheepishly, "I was a day late leaving Denver and then we were robbed coming over Donner Pass."

Stella had big brown eyes, high cheekbones, and a slightly Roman nose. Her hair was long, wavy, and hickory-colored, and her flawless complexion was olive. Stella was a tall, graceful woman, full-breasted, who laughed easily and made Longarm laugh as well. You couldn't help but be attracted to Stella, and when she looked at a man, he'd have to be half dead not to feel his heartbeat quicken.

"What happened to your face!" she exclaimed, holding him out at arm's reach. "Have you already been in a fight?"

"It wasn't much of one," he told her. "Marshal Walker asked me to join his posse. We were fortunate enough to catch the train robbers and put an end to that gang."

As if to prove his point, Longarm pulled out his Ingersoll watch and gold chain. "You see, they took this from me at gunpoint so I really had no choice but to help out a little."

"I bet more than a little," Stella said, taking his arm. "Come inside! I'll pour you a drink and fix you dinner!"

"Sounds good," Longarm told her as she escorted him into a marble-floored hallway and then into a richly appointed parlor. "You have a beautiful home, Stella."

"It pleases me if it pleases you," she said graciously. "I bought this house four years ago from a man who was dying of a cancer and didn't care if he made his neighbors angry by selling it to a saloon owner and former madam."

Longarm studied the shelves of books. "Have you become a reader of literature?"

"Of course not!" She laughed. "*Life* is my teacher. But the former owner had no heirs and so I bought everything including his furniture. I got rid of many things—but not his books. He was a painter—but without talent. So I gave his paintings away to a charity and imported my own from San Francisco. They are all original oils. Do you like them?"

He did not really, because they tended to be mostly vases with flowers and birds on the wing. The sort of thing a woman could appreciate more than a man.

Stella had a small but very fancy bar constructed in one corner of the parlor, and she poured them each a tumbler of her best brandy.

"What shall we toast to?" she asked.

"To you and your future husband. May you have a long and happy life together."

"Thank you," she said, touching their glasses together in salute as they both downed their drinks. Stella poured another and then motioned for Longarm to have a seat. "You look a little tired, Custis."

"I am," he admitted. "But Marshal Walker and I were

able to either capture or kill all the train robbers, so I feel it was worth the time and the effort.''

"I heard that Mark Quaid was killed.''

"He was,'' Longarm said. "I shouldn't have let the hot-headed fool go ahead alone.''

"I wouldn't lose any sleep over it,'' Stella said. "Quaid was always looking for trouble. It was just a matter of time before he got himself killed.''

"That's what Marshal Walker said.'' Longarm drew a cheroot from his pocket. "Do you mind?''

"I never have before, have I?''

"No,'' Longarm said, "but then, I've never visited you in a *respectable* house before, have I?''

Stella laughed. "A woman like me can never hope to hide her past, and I don't even try. Still, it is causing a lot of trouble for Noah.''

"So I heard.''

"I suppose,'' Stella said, "that you heard Noah was supposed to marry someone else.''

"Yes, a Miss Carole Clark. I was told by the town banker that she was the next thing to a saint.''

"Carole looks like an angel, but she has all the warmth of a weasel. She's a back-stabber and the biggest gossip in town. She's also a flirt and has had a number of affairs in San Francisco, but never locally. She's very, very devious. I could have made a lot of money off a girl like her when I had my brothel in Virginia City.''

"I see.''

"On the other hand,'' Stella said, "Noah is exactly as he appears. He is naive, but bighearted and generous to a fault. He'd do anything for a friend. I met him in the local hospital where we both volunteered during a bad epidemic of influenza. We didn't mean to fall in love, but it just happened."

"I'm very happy for you," Longarm said, meaning it.

Stella smiled. "Well," she said, "you know that you're the man that I always intended to marry."

"Stella!"

"Oh, let's not kid ourselves," Stella said. "We were perfect in bed and well matched in temperament. The only problem was that you couldn't trade in your badge for a business suit and I didn't want to be a young widow."

"I'm still alive and have no plans to be otherwise."

Stella's smile faded. "Sooner or later, someone will backshoot you, Custis. Nobody wins all the time. Everyone's luck runs out sooner or later."

"It's not luck," Longarm argued. "I'm good and I am very careful."

"Yeah," she said, obviously not convinced that those attributes would always continue to keep Longarm alive. "Noah is coming over for dinner tonight. You'll like him."

"I look forward to meeting him. How are the wedding plans?"

Stella shrugged. "We've had some problems, I'm afraid. Noah's father has done everything to stop this wedding except to offer a reward to have me shot on sight."

"He must be extremely ambitious."

"Oh, he is!" Stella laughed without humor. "And if you think he's bad, just wait until you meet Nick Huffington!"

"Marshal Walker has already filled me in on him," Longarm said. "I guess he's pure poison."

"The man is a snake! I don't know how Noah escaped being like his father or brother. Maybe God or some divine force thought that there ought to be some balance in the family so they created my Noah."

"Well," Longarm said, puffing on his cheroot and refilling his glass, "I just hope that you and Noah can put all that aside and be happy. Will you stay in Auburn?"

"No. We've both decided to leave this area and start fresh. I think I've got a buyer for my saloon so that, even if Noah is disinherited, we'll still have a good nest egg and be able to build a future."

"You must love him very much."

"I do," she said. "And I can't wait to get married and leave this town where tongues never stop wagging and fingers never stop pointing. Where I'm the evil witch and Miss Carole Clark is an angel. I'm just sick of the whole sorry mess."

"It will be a shame to leave this beautiful house."

"Yes," she said, taking a deep breath and forcing herself to relax. "I do love this home and even Auburn itself. It's just that I can't abide the self-righteousness of some of its people. The ones that call the shots and decide who wins and who loses in Auburn."

"You mean like Mr. Haley, the banker."

"Exactly! You've met him? I'll bet he gave you an earful."

"He did," Longarm admitted. "I had to be rather . . . abrupt with Mr. Haley. I don't think he admires me either."

Longarm and Stella talked for the rest of the afternoon, catching up on old friends and acquaintances. Longarm heard a cook banging around in the kitchen and learned that Stella also kept a maid.

"We're having beef stew, dumplings, and apple pie for dessert," Stella told him about six o'clock. "I hope you have a good appetite."

"I do."

"Have you found a hotel yet?"

"No."

"Good! You can stay here because I have several extra bedrooms."

"I can't do that!"

"Why not?"

"The tongues are wagging fast enough already," Longarm said. "And I don't want to give them any more fodder for gossip. You're about to become a married woman, Stella, and you have to start considering these things, no matter where you and Noah go to start over fresh."

"But my maid is living here with me! She's about sixty and . . ."

"Thanks, Stella, but no, thanks."

"All right."

Just then, they heard a knock at the door. Stella jumped up saying, "It's Noah. I know the sound of his knock."

Longarm came to his feet and prepared to greet Stella's fiancé in the hope of making a good first impression. He thought the world of Stella, and he wanted to also become good friends with Noah.

Noah wasn't anything like Longarm had expected. Stella had always liked big, handsome men, but Noah was only about five feet ten and quite slender and ordinary-looking. He wore glasses and was clean-shaven. When he stuck his hand out to shake with Longarm, he smiled broadly and squinted.

"My pleasure, Marshal Long. I've already heard a good deal about you from Stella, and more recently from members of the posse that went after those train robbers."

"We had a little luck."

"That's not what I heard."

Longarm shifted uncomfortably and turned the topic away from himself. "I want to offer you my heartiest congratulations on your upcoming marriage. Stella and I have been friends for a good many years and, frankly, I am jealous."

Noah had a nice, healthy laugh. "I'd rather you were just envious, Marshal. But anyway, we're being put to the test, aren't we, darling."

"You can say that again," Stella replied. "Are you hungry?"

"I'm always hungry," Noah answered.

Longarm followed the couple into the dining room, where Stella's cook had already prepared the table. They sat down and had another toast to the wedding and then began to enjoy their dinner.

"Noah," Longarm said, "I understand that you and Stella have decided to leave Auburn."

"That's right," he answered. "I'd like to stay in the gold country, but Stella sort of favors moving to San Francisco."

"Either way," Longarm said, "you could hardly go wrong. Will you be starting a new ministry?"

"I'd like to." Noah shook his head. "I just don't know. So much has happened here that I think we both need some time to just relax and enjoy ourselves. I've even thought of getting a little farm down in the San Joaquin Valley. The soil is so rich down there that you can't hardly help but prosper."

Longarm could not imagine Stella Vacarro being a farmer's wife, but he wisely chose not to voice his concerns.

Stella spoke instead. "Noah wonders if we need to move farther away in order to smooth his father's feathers."

"Now Stella, that's not all of it."

"But it's a big part of it," Stella argued. "You're afraid

that if we stay anywhere near Sacramento, you will ruin your father's chances of being elected our next governor. But the truth is, you ought to be worrying about Nick—not us.''

"Stella, please," Noah pleaded. "I'd rather not bore your friend with our family problems. All right?"

"All right," she said, even managing a smile.

Longarm went right on with his dinner. He was ravenous, and had two helpings of stew and probably half the apple pie. And later, when they retired back to the parlor, the heavy meal and the long chase into the Sierras got the better of him and he became very sleepy.

"I'd better be getting to a hotel room," he said, pushing himself to his feet with a yawn. "I'll see you both tomorrow."

"Good night," Noah said, coming to his feet. "Actually, I should go too. I'll walk back with you into town."

"Are you sure?"

"Yes, I have an early appointment," Noah said.

He gave Stella a peck on the cheek and they both left Stella's house a few minutes later. It was dark out, and Longarm figured it was around ten o'clock. He was dead on his feet as they strolled back toward the main part of town and its collection of hotels, saloons, and businesses.

"You think a great deal of Stella, don't you," Noah said, breaking a comfortable silence.

"I do," Longarm admitted. "The woman has character and heart."

"I think so too. I know that she has had a rather . . . sordid past. But that doesn't matter to me. It's what she is *now* that matters, not what she used to be."

"No one ever gave Stella a thing in life," Longarm said. "She's got her tough side, but the miracle is that she didn't become hard and cynical. She's still one of the kindest, most generous women I've ever met. And she's still one of the most beautiful.''

"She's so beautiful that I worry about her," Noah admitted. "I mean, I'm no Adonis. I'm just a real ordinary gent who will probably go bald and chubby in another ten years. I'm afraid that she might . . . might become ashamed of me.''

"No!''

"You don't think so?''

"Of course not! Stella likes what you are *inside*. And that's by far the most important thing." Longarm clapped the much smaller man on his shoulder. "Noah, don't you worry about Stella ever leaving you. Loyalty is one of her greatest qualities. She's in love with you!''

"Thank you!" he said, looking very relieved. "I really can't express how much better I feel having heard you say that. My father and brother and just about everyone else in Auburn have been saying that I'm crazy to marry Stella. But they don't know her like we know her, do they.''

"No," Longarm said, "they do not. Stella is the kind of woman that will make you an even better man. She wants a family and she wants to make the world a little better place than it would have been without her. I sense that you feel the same way.''

"And you as well, Marshal! Why, if I . . .''

Noah Huffington didn't get to finish because his words were interrupted by a rolling volley of gunfire and then shouting.

Longarm grabbed his six-gun and started to run quickly leaving Noah Huffington behind. The shooting could only mean that a lynch mob had attacked the jail and Marshal Walker was in big, big trouble.

Chapter 7

As soon as Longarm rounded the corner, he saw at least fifty men with torches dragging Marshal Walker's five prisoners up the street. Longarm didn't know how they had gotten past Marshal Walker, but he knew that the mob must have used force.

"What happened!" he yelled to an old man that he overtook and spun around.

"We're gonna lynch them bastards!" the old fella exclaimed as he hobbled after the raucous crowd. "Gonna take 'em up to the park and hang 'em in the trees!"

"What about Marshal Walker!"

"They shot the fool!"

"Damn!" Longarm swore, running on down the street as fast as his long legs would carry him.

He didn't stop until he burst into the marshal's office and saw Walker lying on the floor in a pool of blood. He was surrounded by several of his friends, none of whom seemed to know what to do other than to appear stricken and confused.

"Marshal Long!" a middle-aged woman cried hysterically. "They've *shot* him!"

Longarm dropped down on his knees and grabbed Walker's wrist. "He's still alive. Has someone sent for a doctor?"

"Yes," the woman answered. "He should be here any minute. But our marshal is bleeding to death!"

Longarm tore off his coat, then his shirt, which he proceeded to tear into strips. The marshal had been shot twice, once in the shoulder and once in the head. He'd lost a lot of blood and his color was pasty white. His pulse was faint, and Longarm thought the man could die at any minute and that the most critical need was to stop the bleeding.

The slug had gone completely through the shoulder so that the only thing that Longarm could do was to pack cloth into both the entry and exit wounds to staunch the bleeding. He'd done it more than once before and wasn't a bit squeamish about the matter. Several of the marshal's friends, however, vigorously protested the rough but necessary treatment.

"That isn't going to do anything!" one man cried. "It's the head wound that will kill him!"

"Shut up or go outside and wait for the doctor!" Longarm ordered as he used his longer strips to cinch down his crude plugs. Then he turned his attention to the more critical head wound.

"Is he going to live?" the woman asked. "Has he any chance at all!"

"I don't know," Longarm answered. "The head wound might not be as bad as I first thought. If that's the case, our friend could survive."

"It was awful the way they took those train robbers and rapists," the woman said. "That lynch mob isn't much better

70

than the ones they took from this jail! They were drunk—
real drunk, and howling for blood like a pack of winter-
starved wolves. Poor Pete tried to stop them. He had a shotgun and threatened to use it. But someone—I can't imagine
who—shot him down right in front of this office! It was
awful!"

"Yeah," Longarm said, "I've seen it happen a time or
two before. There's something about a lynching that brings
out the very devil in normally law-abiding men."

The woman shook her head and tears slid down her
cheeks. "When Pete fell, they trampled right over the top of
him like he was nothing," she said. "They found the cell
keys and dragged those five prisoners out and started to beat
them. I was outside and we could hear the prisoners scream-
ing. Next thing I knew, they were dragging the prisoners out
and then down the street. I think they were already half
dead."

"Where is that doctor!" Longarm swore as he wrapped
strips of his shirt around Walker's head until it looked as if
the lawman was wearing a crimson turban.

Longarm ached to jump up and race down toward the park
in an attempt to save the prisoners, but he wasn't about to
leave Marshal Walker until the doctor arrived.

"Most of 'em were wearing hoods," another one of Walker's friends in attendance offered. "But they weren't hard to
pick out. I recognized Mr. Haley right away."

"That figures. Who else?"

"The mayor as well as most everyone of the city council."

"And Deacon Phillips!"

"Really?" the woman asked. "Are you sure!"

"I am, and—"

"Stand back!" the doctor shouted as he pushed inside and

then dropped to one knee next to Pete Walker. Like Longarm, the first thing he did was to take Pete Walker's pulse. Then he thumbed back Pete's eyelids to study the lawman's pupils. After that, he made a quick inspection of Longarm's bandaging work and said, "What have we got here?"

"I think the bullet that struck his head creased bone and tore off the top of his ear," Longarm said. "But I don't think it pierced the skull."

"Let's find out," the doctor said, quickly removing the bandage, then using a clean bandage to wipe the wound. Longarm realized he was holding his breath as the doctor ran his index finger along the welling crease in Walker's scalp.

"Well?"

"You're right. He could bleed to death from this, but there shouldn't be any brain damage. What about the shoulder? Did the bullet hit him in the lung?"

"Not that I could tell," Longarm said. "I've seen a few men that were lung-shot, and he doesn't look or sound like one to me. Also, the bullet passed through the shoulder. I tried to stop the bleeding on both sides, but I'm not sure that I entirely succeeded."

"Hmmm," the doctor mused as he placed a stethoscope to Walker's chest and listened closely to the man's breathing. "Sounds normal."

The doctor pushed himself to his feet. He was old enough to have had a lot of experience, but young enough to have attended a real school of medicine back in the East. Longarm quickly judged him to be both decisive and knowledgeable.

"Marshal, we need to get Pete over to my office just a few doors away where I can patch him up as quickly as possible. Can you help me carry him?"

"Sure," Longarm said, still wanting to try to save the five train robbers for a jury.

"You're bigger and stronger than I am," the doctor said. "Let's grab one of those blankets on the bunk, lay him on it, and pick up the ends. We can sort of lug him over to my surgery as if he were lying in a hammock."

"Dr. Davis, I'll help you," the older woman said. "I'm stronger than I look."

"Thanks, Mabel" the doctor said, "but I think it would be easier on our friend if just the federal marshal and I did it together. If Pete were accidentally dropped, it could prove fatal."

They carefully placed the unconscious marshal on a blanket, and twisted up both ends so that he really was in a hammock. Then, with Longarm hoisting the heavier end, they carried Walker outside and a few doors up the sidewalk to the doctor's office. Longarm could hear the lynch mob shouting and raising hell just a block or two away.

"You don't want to be there anyway," Davis said as they laid the marshal down for a moment so he could open his door. "You couldn't stop that mob. If they'd shoot Marshal Walker, they'd certainly do the same to you."

"I suppose," Longarm said grimly. "But this sure doesn't sit well with me."

"It doesn't sit well with any of us," Davis reminded him. "I've lived in Auburn for over ten years and this is only the second lynching I've seen. But I'm afraid that, with Marshal Walker down, it might not be the last. There is a lawless element here that will quickly take things over."

"Not if I have anything to say about it," Longarm replied.

They struggled inside, and somehow managed to hoist Walker up on a small operating table.

"Anything more that I can do?" Longarm asked.

"Don't go down to the park," the doctor warned. "Just wait here and—"

"I can't just wait here," Longarm said, "any more than you could if you saw a dying man, no matter how evil he might be."

"Yes," Davis agreed, "I see your point. But this town is about to become completely at the mercy of its worst element. Marshal Quaid is dead. Marshal Walker is out of commission, maybe even dying. And if you get killed, well . . ."

But Longarm wasn't listening as he headed outside and then began to run down the street toward the park. It was quite likely that the hanging party was already over, but he had to find out for himself and damn the consequences. As he ran, he could hear the shouting and the sound of gunfire, and asked himself what one man could possibly do to stop what was happening. Probably nothing, but he figured he had to try.

The park was ablaze with uplifted torches, and it was a scene straight from Hell. Three of the prisoners were still violently kicking their way into eternity, their necks twisted at grotesque angles. Their hands had been tied behind their backs, but their legs were loose and churning madly as if they were trying to outrun Satan himself.

Noah Huffington was standing in a wagon bed, pleading for the crowd to stop the lynching and to spare the last two prisoners, who were groveling in the dirt, shaking with terror.

"This is *wrong*!" Noah shouted. "Without benefit of a trial, this is *murder*! Please don't hang these other two men! Haven't we seen enough death already!"

But the lynch mob wasn't nearly satisfied. If anything, the gruesome sight of the three men thrashing wildly at the end of their ropes, faces purple and bloated, eyes bulging and mouths distended in silent screams, acted to fuel their dark passions.

Longarm drew his six-gun and slammed into the crowd as the mob berated Noah Huffington, and then someone hurled an empty whiskey bottle that struck the young minister flush in the face and knocked him down into the wagon.

Longarm bowled people over as he surged through the crowd toward the three hanged men. He grabbed a big hunting knife from a man's belt and cut the nearest train robber down, knowing that the outlaw's neck was broken and that he was already dead.

Before he could reach the other two, the bloodthirsty mob roared like a single, mindless animal. Longarm pistol-whipped an attacker, then spun him around to use as a shield. He placed his pistol against the unconscious man's temple and shouted, "Enough or I'll kill him and open fire on all of you!"

The crowd was drunk . . . but not so drunk that it couldn't see that Longarm wasn't bluffing. It pulsed with hatred and men cursed and screamed, but no one dared to accept Longarm's challenge.

"Disperse!" Longarm shouted. "I'm a United States marshal! Mayor Yarrow, damn you! Get up here!"

Yarrow had removed his hood, just like many of the others. Now, as the other two hanged prisoners stiffened in death, the mayor sheepishly stepped forward.

"Tell these *good* citizens of yours that I'll call in the United States Army and have this whole damned town put under arrest if this crowd doesn't disperse!"

"All right, folks," Yarrow said, "this man is a United States marshal and things have gotten out of hand. We all know that these other two will hang, but let's show the government that we are law-abiding citizens. Let's go home."

The mob grumbled, but they slowly turned and headed back to the saloons. Longarm figured the trouble was over. He dropped the man he held as a shield and jumped up into the back of the wagon.

"Noah? Are you all right?"

Huffington sat up looking groggy. "What hit me?"

"A whiskey bottle," Longarm told him. "That crowd was so bloodthirsty that you're lucky they didn't hang *you*."

"Did they hang all the prisoners?"

"Three of them are dead. The other two are wishing they were already dead. It's over."

"Is Marshal Walker alive?"

"Barely," Longarm said, helping the man down from the wagon. "Are you able to walk?"

"Yeah, I'll survive," Noah said, holding his face, "but I'm not going to look so good for my wedding."

"You'll look fine," Longarm said even as he noted how rapidly one side of Noah Huffington's face was swelling. "Now, I'd better collect these two living prisoners and get them back to jail."

"Noah!"

It was Stella and she had a gun in her hand as she came racing across the park. "Custis! Are you all right?"

"A little worse for wear," Noah said, opening his arms for Stella. "But I'm fine . . . thanks to your friend."

"Think nothing of it," Longarm said, "but I'm glad that you have both decided to leave after your wedding. I'm afraid that we *both* made some enemies tonight."

"No loss considering the nature of that bunch," Noah said.

76

"Well," Longarm answered, "I'm sure that you're right, but just be careful for a few days until things cool down. I'll be taking up residence at the jail until we can get a judge, jury, and a trial over with. Or until I can find someone else to replace Marshal Walker."

"Can you really stay that long?" Stella asked.

"I'll have to," Longarm said. "First thing in the morning I'll get a telegram off to my boss in Denver telling him the situation. I'm sure he'll understand. We're Feds, but we still have an obligation to step in and preserve local law when there is no local authority left standing."

Stella nodded and kissed his cheek. "Thanks, Custis. Thanks a lot! You couldn't have given me a better wedding present than to keep Noah from being seriously hurt . . . or killed."

"Just watch out for him, Stella. I saw a lot of hatred in that mob and I expect it to last a while. So be careful."

"We will. You too!"

"Count on it," Longarm said as he hauled the two fallen prisoners to their feet and prodded them back toward the jail.

Chapter 8

Longarm had a troubled night. Several times, members of the lynch mob came by the marshal's office to curse and taunt him into stepping out into the street, but Longarm ignored them and kept the front door bolted shut. He drifted off to sleep just before morning, and didn't awaken until nine o'clock when there was a pounding at the door.

"Marshal Long! It's Doc Davis. Open up!"

Longarm rolled off the bunk and hurried to the front door, which he unbolted. Dr. Davis looked very haggard, but he had a smile on his face.

"How is Marshal Walker?" Longarm asked as he let the man inside and quickly closed and bolted the door behind him.

"Pete is a fighter and I think he will pull through. My main concern is that he doesn't contract a brain infection."

"That's fine news."

"How are you and the prisoners holding up?" the doctor asked, looking toward the cells.

"As you can see, they're still sleeping. They're pretty badly shaken, but otherwise fine."

"The merciful thing might just have been to let them swing," the doctor told him. "I mean . . . I know you're sworn to uphold the law, but given the circumstances, it wasn't worth almost losing Pete Walker."

"It's a matter of principle," Longarm told the physician. "When a good lawman takes an oath to uphold the law, he isn't about to allow a lynch mob to have its way. Our oath of office means as much to Pete and me as your Hippocratic oath does to you."

"Of course it does," Dr. Davis said, "and I apologize for my thoughtless remarks. But I am very concerned about the talk I'm hearing this morning on the streets."

"What are you hearing?"

"I'm hearing no regrets about the lynchings last night— only about the fact that you saved those last two."

"We need to get a judge here right away," Longarm said. "Where would he come from?"

"Sacramento. I have connections in the state capital. Would you like me to send out a few telegraphs informing the governor that we need a judge and some new local authority up here right away?"

"That would be a big help," Longarm said. "I wasn't sure how I was going to send for help and also keep an eye on these prisoners."

"Consider it done," the doctor said. "Do your prisoners need any medical attention?"

"No, but given the certainty of their fate, they could probably use some spiritual comforting."

"Sorry, but that's not my line. I could send someone over to speak to them if . . ."

"Don't bother," Longarm said. "I've seen a lot of men face death, and unless they ask for a man of God, they aren't ready to listen. Just go send that telegram and let's try to keep a tight lid on this town.''

"Miss Vacarro really wanted to come by and visit you this morning,'' the doctor said, "but I told her that might not be such a good idea.''

"It wouldn't be,'' Longarm agreed. "She's already the object of scorn by most of the so-called respectable citizens. Coming here would just give them more ammunition. Tell her that I am fine but that I might not be able to make it to her wedding on Saturday.''

"She's postponed it,'' the doctor said. "Given what happened last night, she told me to tell you that she and Noah have decided to wait another few weeks until things settle down.''

"They ought to just elope,'' Longarm growled. "Stella will never be accepted in Auburn, and I suspect that poor Noah lost a good many friends last night.''

"He sure did,'' Davis agreed. "But I admire him for standing up for what he believes. Although to be honest, I'm convinced that we'd have been better served if all five of the prisoners had been lynched.''

"You'd better get going,'' Longarm said, taking a peek out the window. "After you send the telegrams, see if you can get some food sent over here, but make sure it hasn't been poisoned.''

"I'll do that.''

"And keep me posted about what is going on,'' Longarm added. "Especially on Marshal Walker's condition.''

"I'm more optimistic about that than anything else,'' the doctor said as he opened the door and stepped outside. "*You're* the one that I'm really worried about, Marshal.''

"Don't waste your time worrying about me,'' Longarm

told the man. "Just take care of Walker and those telegrams. Speaking of which, I need to send one to my boss in Denver explaining my predicament and the fact that I will probably be late in returning to work."

"Damned late, I expect."

"Depends on how swift justice works in a California court," Longarm said before he closed the door.

"Hey, Marshal!" one of the prisoners called. "What about some breakfast!"

Longarm went back to stand before the cell, where he studied to two men. They were both in their late twenties or early thirties, and he couldn't help but think about how terrified they'd been the night before while they were groveling in the dirt and waiting for their turn to be hanged.

Longarm grabbed the bars and leaned forward until his face was almost up against the cell. "You know," he said, "you boys have cost me a lot of trouble already. If I hear any complaints, any whatsoever, I may just toss you to the wolves."

"No, you won't," the one who was doing all the talking said. "I overheard you telling Doc all that crap about taking an oath to uphold the law. And I remember what you said to the mob last night." The train robber sneered. "Marshal, you couldn't give us up even if you wanted."

Longarm shrugged. "I guess you're a real bright fella. Got me all figured out and everything."

"You bet I have! And I'm going to *escape* too. Maybe not today, but I won't be hanged."

"What's your name?" Longarm asked.

"Why you want to know?"

"Just thought you might appreciate me sending a note to

tell your family you went kicking your way into Hell at the end of a rope. That's all.''

"You go to Hell!''

Longarm chuckled. ''I guess that means that you got no family, huh? Probably just as well. What about your friend?''

"My name is William Pierce,'' the quiet one said, coming to his feet. ''And I'll give you the names and address of my family and Jack's family on the day we hang.''

"Fair enough, William. You sound like you're from Texas.''

"El Paso,'' the prisoner said. ''And I damn sure wish that I was back there now.''

"You should have thought about that before you started robbing trains and raping innocent passengers.''

"Yeah,'' William said, ''but it was a lot of damned fun while it lasted.''

"You bet it was!'' Jack crowed. ''Them last two girls was—''

"Save it for the judge and jury,'' Longarm warned. ''I don't want to hear about it.''

Jack's eyes widened. He was a big man with a three-day-old beard and wild blue eyes. Cleaned up, he would probably be handsome. But now, covered with dirt and trying to sound tough, he just made Longarm sick.

"I'm *escaping*!'' Jack shouted before turning away. ''Ain't no way that I'm going to be hanged like them three last night. I saw how bad they died. The mob didn't even drop 'em! They just put nooses around their necks and hauled 'em up about three feet into the air. Luke got lucky and his neck broke because he was thrashing around so hard, but Joe and Clancy . . . well, I'd rather take a bullet any old day, Marshal.''

"Yeah," Longarm said, going over to sit with his feet up on Walker's desk. "The only promise I can make is that you'll be properly hanged, not strangled like your friends."

Ten minutes later there was another pounding at the door.

"Who is it!" Longarm called, dropping his feet to the floor.

"It's Lola."

"Who?"

"Lola! I have a message from Marshal Walker."

Longarm remembered that Lola was the beautiful whore that Walker had taken such a shine to that he'd even invited her to come to Auburn. "Just a minute," he said.

He unbolted the door and opened it a crack. It was Lola, all right, and she looked as pretty as a rose with her black hair and slender but curvaceous body.

"What are *you* doing here?" Longarm asked, letting the young woman inside.

"I was over at the doctor's office when Pete woke up. He's real worried about you and wanted to come over, but Dr. Davis wouldn't let him."

"Go back and tell Pete that everything is under control. The best thing he can do is to help get a judge and another marshal here as soon as possible."

"I will tell him," Lola said, glancing past Longarm toward his prisoners. She walked around Longarm to stand in the middle of the office. "I heard that these *pigs* squealed pretty loud last night, eh?"

"Shut up, you whore!" Jack screamed. "If I ever get my hands on you, Lola, I'll make *you* scream!"

Lola spat at the man, and Longarm saw pure hatred transform her pretty face for a moment before she turned on her high heels and walked back to the front door.

"I will go to bring *you* food," she said, "if you have a little money."

Longarm had to smile. He thought it very likely that if he gave Lola any money, she would just spend it on herself. And yet he was famished, and curious whether he was right about her or not.

"All right," he agreed, digging into his pockets and pulling out a few dollars. "Here. We could use a pot of coffee and three breakfasts."

"The hell with them," she said. "I bring *you* food, let them starve!"

"Bring us *all* something," Longarm told her.

She dipped her chin. "Okay. I'll be back soon."

Longarm let her outside saying, "Give my best to Marshal Walker. Tell him I've got things under control here at the jail and just to rest and not worry until he feels strong enough to come and help."

"He's very weak," Lola replied. "The doctor said that he nearly bled to death. That he *would* have bled to death if you hadn't known exactly what to do. But he has a good marshal friend in Placerville. Anyway, he's already had a telegram sent asking him to come over and give you a hand."

"That's the best news I've heard in a while," Longarm said. "And Lola, thanks."

When she smiled, she looked as young, wholesome, and innocent as a schoolgirl. Longarm had a very powerful impulse to touch her, but resisted.

When the door closed, Jack hissed, "So when she comes back with food, why don't we all screw her for a couple of hours, Marshal! Might as well have ourselves some fun while we wait and see what's going to happen next."

"Shut up," Longarm ordered, returning to his chair.

"She's good," Jack persisted. "Lola is just as good as she looks."

Longarm ignored the man. He knew that Jack was trying to get him riled enough to go into the cell, where the prisoner hoped to be able to overpower him and make a desperate bid for freedom. Well, it wasn't going to happen. Maybe that kind of tactic could work with a fool like Marshal Quaid, but not with Longarm.

Nearly an hour passed before Lola returned with a big picnic basket of hot food and a pot of strong black coffee. Longarm divided the food into thirds. Then he and his prisoners ate hungrily while Lola sat and watched.

When they were finished, Lola collected the cups, plates, and spoons and put them back in the empty basket. "Did you get enough to eat, Marshal Long?"

"It'll hold us until supper. Thanks."

"You're welcome," she said, smiling fetchingly. "Is there *anything* else you need? Anything at all?"

Longarm thought he would thoroughly enjoy a little dessert in the form of Lola, but that was certainly out of the question given the grim circumstances.

"I guess not," he said.

Lola shrugged. "In that case, I had better go."

"Lola?"

"Yes?"

"What is going on in the street? Have things cooled down a little?"

"Yes," Lola told him, tossing her long black hair and leaning against the door. "I haven't been into the saloons, but I doubt there will be any more trouble."

"That's good to hear. I came west to attend a wedding

and to have a vacation. So far, things haven't worked out the way that I'd planned."

"They almost never do," Lola said quietly. "We make plans, have dreams and . . . well, it is all foolishness, isn't it?"

There was such sadness in her voice that Longarm did reach out this time and lay his hand on her shoulder. "What happened to *your* bright dreams, Lola? How did you wind up in some abandoned mining town selling yourself to train robbers, murderers, and rapists?"

Instead of answering, Lola left the office calling out over her shoulder, "Don't worry, Marshal Long. I'll be back with something to eat for supper."

"Then you'll need some more money!" Longarm reached back into his pocket, but Lola was already striding down the boardwalk.

Longarm watched her hips swing with exaggerated, professional ease. Men riding horses down the center of the street reined up short and gaped. Pedestrians stopped in their tracks, then turned to watch with hungry smiles. Hell, even male dogs wagged their damn tails furiously and licked their lips.

Longarm closed the door and went back to his chair.

"So she's coming back tonight with supper, huh?" Jack said. "Well, well! Now that ought to give us something to look forward to, huh, Marshal!"

"Yeah," Longarm said, "it will."

"Want to play some poker between the bars?"

"No."

"Then what the hell are we going to do all day?"

"Just wait and see what happens," Longarm told his prisoner. "And then wait some more."

"Yeah," Jack said in a sarcastic tone of voice, "that's what lawmen have always done best, isn't it. The rest of the world is working its ass off, and the man with the badge just *sits* on his ass all day."

Longarm glanced over at the prisoner. "William?"

"Yeah?"

"Tell your partner in crime that if he doesn't shut up, neither one of you are going to eat again before tomorrow morning."

William looked up at the bigger, younger, and stronger man, then back at Longarm. "You'd better tell him yourself, Marshal. He won't listen to me."

"I think he's got the message," Longarm said with a yawn as he went over to the front window, then pulled the curtain aside to survey the street.

Auburn was quiet, with only normal activity. It looked like a nice, peaceful frontier town, which made it easy to forget what had happened only the night before.

"Think I'll take a nap," Longarm said, trudging over to the bunk and stretching out with a yawn.

The prisoners stretched out on their own bunks. Jack belched loudly and then pulled his hat over his face. He was snoring in a very few minutes.

William came over to press his face against the bars and whisper, "Marshal, there isn't any chance of us getting life in prison instead of the gallows, is there?"

"There's always a chance," Longarm replied, glancing over at the man, "but I'd be lying if I said it was a good one."

"I didn't even kill anyone."

"But you were part of the robbery and you probably raped along with the others."

"I did," William confessed, his eyes growing damp. "I don't know why either. I got two sisters about the same age as the young women we dragged off the trains. And after we did 'em, I felt like dirt. Lower than dirt. I felt like shit. Robbing folks is one thing, rapin' decent girls is another. I got no right to ask for mercy, but I sure can't stand the thought of dying either."

"We all die sometime," Longarm told the man.

"But I'm only thirty-two years old! I ain't lived but half my natural life. And what I have lived has been hard, low, and mean. I never had a chance. That's why I started to run with outlaws when I was real young. That's why I'm in this awful fix right now."

"Oh, horseshit!" Longarm snapped, adjusting his pillow. "You had to have met a lot of good men while you were growing up. Men that had honor and decency and worked from sunup until sundown trying to do the best they could with the hand they were dealt. Men who didn't take the wrong fork in the road just because life was tough."

William sniffled. "Yeah, I met a lot of 'em. When I was younger, I used to think they were as dumb as the mules they followed in the fields. That they were fools . . . and worse. Now I know that *I* was the real fool. And my foolishness is going to cost me my poor, miserable life."

"I'm afraid that is so, William," Longarm agreed, without a shred of pity. "But why don't you just stop thinking about that and get some rest."

"I'll soon be resting in Hell."

"Take a nap, William. And, if you can't do that, at least let me take one for you."

"You're a tough man, Marshal Long. Real tough. You got

the badge, but you got no pity. You're like Jack here. He's got no pity either.''

"You're wrong, William. You were wrong about the hard-working men you judged to be as dumb as mules, and you're wrong about me. I do have pity, but I don't waste it on outlaws like you and Jack and the three that were lynched last night. You'll all get what you have coming.''

"And what do *you* have coming!'' William cried as he wiped tears from his cheeks and struggled to keep from sobbing.

Longarm thought about that for only a second, then replied, "A nap today, a vacation tomorrow. Now shut up, William, before I have to come into that cell and *put* you to sleep.''

William took a long, ragged breath. "You'd love to do that, wouldn't you, Marshal Long. You'd enjoy coming in here and beating the shit out of me. Maybe pistol-whipping me across the head a few times and then doing the same to Jack. You'd like to see us bleed today, wouldn't you!''

"Shut up, William. I'm going to sleep now.''

"You lawmen are all the same,'' William choked. "You got the badge, but you're no different than those of us who crossed to the other side and broke the rules. There just ain't a single cent's worth of difference between you and me!''

"Yeah, there is,'' Longarm told the ranting prisoner. "The difference is that I'm going on vacation and you're going to the gallows.''

Longarm pulled his hat over his eyes. With a big breakfast under his belt, no sign of trouble out in the street, and a long, boring day ahead of him, taking a nap seemed like the most sensible thing to do.

•   •   •

If was early afternoon when he awoke to a loud pounding at the door. Longarm was sleeping so soundly that he came up grabbing for his gun and dazedly looking for an attack. But he quickly recovered and hurried to the door.

"Who is it!"

"Stella! Open up, Custis! Please open up!"

Longarm opened the door and Stella threw herself into his arms, sobbing. He held her tightly for a few minutes and then he said, "So Marshal Walker didn't make it, huh?"

"That's not it, Custis!"

"Then . . . then what?"

"Noah has been murdered!"

Longarm eased Stella back to arm's length and studied her face. "Stella, are you sure?"

"Yes. And they think *I* killed him!"

"What?"

"Oh, Custis, it's true! They're going to hang me like they did those three men last night!"

Before Longarm could react, a rifle boomed from across the street and Stella crumpled into his arms.

"Stella!" he shouted, kicking the door shut and then throwing the bolt as another slug bit into the thick wood. "Stella!"

The ambusher had missed the mark. Stella had only been grazed across the neck. Blood oozed from her flesh wound, and she clamped her hand over it.

"Custis, am I going to die?"

"No," he promised, yanking his bandanna out of his pocket and pressing it to the wound as another shot shattered the silence out in the street. "You're going to be all right."

He got Stella back on her feet and over to his bunk. "Just hold that bandanna to your neck and keep it pressed tight,"

91

Longarm ordered as he dashed back to the window, gun in hand.

But the street was empty. The ambusher was nowhere to be seen.

Longarm hurried back to Stella. She was crying as he pulled the bandanna away to inspect the wound. "It's not bad," he assured her. "You'll have a nasty scar, but nothing more."

In reply, Stella reached up and gripped his shirt. "Dammit, don't you understand! Someone murdered Noah and they think it was *me*!"

"But . . . but why!"

"Because they . . . they found my stiletto in his back, that's why!"

Longarm groaned. Given Stella Vacarro's checkered past, it was easy to see why the crowd immediately assumed she had murdered her well-liked fiancé. And with Stella's stiletto buried in poor Noah Huffington's back, of course everyone would believe she was guilty beyond any reasonable doubt.

"Custis, what am I going to do! I've got to run and hide!"

She tried to get up, but he held her down. "That's just exactly what whoever *really* murdered Noah wants you to do. Stella, if you run, they'll catch you and string you up. I can't leave here to help you. You have to stay with me."

"Stay here? In this jail?"

"That's right," Longarm told her. "It's the only place where you've got a chance until we can figure out a way to prove your innocence."

"But . . ."

"Stella! You've got to trust me! Someone managed to get your weapon and use it to murder Noah. And that someone is *hoping* you panic and run. Don't you see that!"

"Yes," she whispered. "Yes!"

"It's all going to be fine," Longarm said, knowing how hollow his words sounded.

"No, it's not! I *loved* Noah! We were going to be married! Have children. Make a family and spend the rest of our lives together! That's all gone now."

"I'm sorry," Longarm said. "I liked Noah. All I can do is protect you and then find out who really murdered him."

"Maybe it was his father." Tears streamed down Stella's cheeks. "Or his evil brother or someone in politics or . . . I don't know!"

Longarm didn't know either. But he vowed to find out. Now, however, he heard the mob coming back down the street. And this time, they were coming for Stella.

Longarm jumped up and hurried over to the rifle rack. He grabbed a double-barreled shotgun that was already loaded. He jammed a fistful of shells into his pockets and checked his side arm.

"Why don't you let us out to help you fight!" Jack screamed. "You can't stand them all off! They'll do the same to you as they did to that old marshal! Let us out!"

"Not a chance!" Longarm grated.

Stella pushed herself up and staggered across the office, still holding the bloody bandage to her neck. She went to the rifle rack and pulled out the other shotgun, then loaded it as if she did so every day.

"What are you doing!" Longarm shouted. "Get back on that bunk!"

"No. If we're going to die, we'll die together, Custis. I'm not taking this lying down!"

Stella's lovely face was very pale and she was unsteady on her feet. Longarm could see that Stella wasn't going to back down from anyone or anything. Blood was trickling down her neck to stain her dress, but she didn't care.

As Longarm took his position behind the door, he glanced over at Stella and felt very proud just to be her friend.

Chapter 9

"Marshal Long, open up! It's Lola!"

"Go away!" he shouted.

"I have food! Open up!"

Longarm could see another mob gathering in the street, and he was afraid that some drunken fool might mistake Lola for Stella and open fire, killing her at his doorstep. "All right," he said, unbolting the door and opening it just enough for Lola to squeeze inside. "You shouldn't have come here."

But Lola wasn't listening. Her eyes were on Stella. The two women studied each other for a long moment. Then Stella said, "Why *did* you risk your life coming here?"

"To be with Custis, of course." Lola stared at the bloody bandanna that Stella was holding to her neck. "Have you been shot?"

"I thought that you were *Pete's* friend," Stella said, ignoring the question.

Lola shook her head, and then she turned and gave Longarm a brilliant smile. "This is the man I really want."

Longarm stepped between them. "Stop it, the both of you," he said roughly. "Lola, you're the only one that

95

doesn't need to be here in case things get really ugly. I want you to leave."

Lola shook her head, then motioned to the rifle rack. "I can shoot a pistol or rifle. Maybe you need my help."

"No," Longarm told her. "But if you really want to help, then you should go tell Marshal Walker and Dr. Davis what is happening. See if there is help on the way. Send another telegram. If we don't get some help here pretty soon, I'm afraid that that lynch mob is going to just get drunk again and make another attempt to storm this jail."

"I'll go," Lola said, starting for the door. "If necessary, I'll send a telegram for help myself, although I do not know anyone to send it to."

"There must be a judge and some lawmen closer to Auburn than Sacramento. See if you can find them! Tell them that we're going to go down fighting before I'll allow Stella or my last two prisoners to be lynched."

"I'll tell them," Lola promised, setting another basketful of food on the desk and starting to leave. At the door, however, she stopped and turned. "Miss Vacarro, who *really* killed your fiancé?"

"I don't know."

"They say it was your knife that was buried in his back. They say it was a double-edged stiletto."

"That knife was stolen from me almost six months ago," Stella said. "Maybe by the one who murdered poor Noah, maybe by someone who just happened to sell it in a pawnshop or saloon. I have no idea, but I did not—could not—ever murder the man I loved enough to marry."

"Then you *don't* love Marshal Long?"

Stella started to answer, but then changed her mind. "Why

don't we see if we live long enough to have a nice, long talk someday? All right?''

''All right,'' Lola said with a nod before she slipped back outside.

When Longarm bolted the door again, Stella said, ''You attract women like bees to honey, Custis. You always have.''

''Can we talk about something serious?'' he asked shortly. ''There's a lynch mob starting to gather outside. It's pretty tame right now, but I can tell you that it will get wilder and wilder as the afternoon wears on. And by nightfall, we're going to have them howling in the street for your blood, my blood, and the blood of our two train robbers.''

''You got to let us defend ourselves!'' Jack shouted from behind the bars. ''Marshal Long, if they storm in here like they did last night, you and that woman sure ain't gonna be able to stop them!''

''Maybe not, but I'll go down trying.''

''That's not good enough!'' Jack screamed. ''We need to arm ourselves!''

''Not a chance,'' Longarm sternly told the prisoner. ''We're just going to sit tight and wait because I know that help is on the way.''

''And if it ain't?''

''Then I'll fight,'' Longarm gritted out.

''No,'' Stella corrected, ''we'll *both* fight.''

''Yeah,'' Longarm said, not even wanting to think about the possibility of standing side by side with Stella against a blood-crazed lynch mob.

Two hours passed like two days, and then there was another loud pounding on the door.

''Maybe it's the doctor or some help,'' Longarm said,

jumping up from his chair and drawing his six-gun. He walked up to the door and yelled, "Who is it!"

"Abe Huffington! Open up, Marshal Long!"

"Why?"

"My son and I want to talk things over!"

Stella said, "You can't trust either of them, but what have we got to lose?"

"I agree," Longarm said.

He turned to the door and shouted, "All right. Disarm yourselves and put your hands over your heads."

A short argument between Abe and Nick Huffington took place, but the older man cut it short and then yelled, "All right! We're not packing any hideout weapons. Open up this damned door!"

"Stella," Longarm ordered, "keep your shotgun trained on them all the time."

"Don't worry about that," she told him as she backed to the wall. "I know better than anyone that they're as deadly as a pair of vipers."

Longarm unbolted the door and eased it open. He saw a big, jowly man in a gray suit with a derby hat who was glaring hatefully at him. That would be Abe. Nick was shorter and leaner with a hard cut to his features. His eyes were bloodshot and he seemed to be having difficulty focusing.

"Come on in," Longarm said, backing up. "And close the door behind you."

Abe marched inside. He smelled heavily of cologne, but also of whiskey, and he wore full muttonchop whiskers and had an air of importance as well as impatience. His eyes raked over Longarm and then shot across the room to Stella.

"You!" Abe hissed. "I *knew* that you were poison! I

98

warned Noah that no good would come of his association with a whore like you!''

"I didn't kill him!" Stella shouted with the shotgun wavering in her fists. "I think *you* did!"

"What?" Abe took a menacing step toward Stella, but Longarm grabbed the older man by the arm. Nick started to jump at him, but Longarm whipped up his six-gun and growled, "You wouldn't want to leave your father without *any* sons, now would you?"

Nick got the message. His lip curled with contempt as he tried to focus on Stella. "You dirty whore! You—"

Longarm's gun swept upward and slammed against the side of Nick's head, splitting his temple and dropping the younger man to his knees.

"Damn you, Marshal!" Abe roared. "You're going to pay for this outrage!"

"Why don't you just sit down."

Abe unbuttoned his expensive suit coat and sat. He looked down at Nick without sympathy and then back up at Longarm. "That Vacarro woman murdered my son Noah sometime last night. The murder weapon was found buried in his back and everyone knows it belonged to Stella! I want her arrested for the murder of my son!"

"All right," Longarm said, glancing over at Stella. "You're under arrest, Miss Vacarro."

She just shrugged, the shotgun still pointed at Abe and Nick.

"Well?" Abe bellowed. "Arrest and throw her in jail!"

"No," Longarm said. "She might come in handy in case you try to incite those fools outside to start up another lynch party tonight."

"Don't you understand? My son has been murdered!"

"And I promise to do everything I can to find out who *really* put that knife in your son's back. I do know that it wasn't Stella. Like yourself, she loved Noah—and he loved her in return."

"Noah didn't know what he was doing!" Abe stormed. "That Vacarro woman put a spell—or an evil hex on my boy. She lied, connived, and tricked him into proposing marriage. She used all her wiles to make him temporarily insane. She only wanted our family money and respectability. And then . . . then, so he wouldn't regain his sanity and call the marriage off, she murdered him!"

"And what proof do you have to support that accusation?" Longarm demanded. "Because you see, even rich and important politicians operate under the same laws as the rest of us commoners. And the United States Constitution guarantees that everyone should be considered innocent until proven guilty by a court of law. As a successful politician, you more than anyone else ought to know that."

Huffington shook himself like a big, wet dog, and then got a firm grip on his composure. He knelt beside Nick and said, "Stand up, boy! You're going to live and I'll make damn sure that this man loses his badge."

"Mr. Huffington," Longarm said, "despite what you think of Stella's morals and motives, doesn't it seem a little odd to you that she would murder the man that you are saying would have guaranteed her your family money and respectability? Why wouldn't she have waited until *after* the marriage? As it is now, she has no legal claim to your family estate. None whatsoever."

"I didn't need their money!" Stella angrily interrupted. "I never wanted a cent of it and neither did Noah. I have money of my own! Plenty of it! And I damn sure wouldn't have been so stupid as to have killed Noah and then left my own knife as evidence.''

"She makes sense," Longarm said to the grief-stricken man. "If anyone had a motive for killing Noah, it was you, Nick."

Nick tried to stand. Failing that, he said, "I'll get you for this, Marshal! You're going to pay!"

"Shut up, Nick," said Abe.

"I'll *kill* him!"

"Nick, shut up."

Nick grabbed the edge of the desk and pulled himself unsteadily to his feet. A big bump was already forming on the side of his head, and Longarm could only imagine how badly the man felt. A pistol-whipping on top of a bottle of whiskey could test the physical constitution of any man.

"You're in a bad fix," Abe warned Longarm, "but maybe there is some way that I can solve this dilemma."

"How?" Longarm asked.

"Well," Abe began, "those people outside know and respect me and my family. If you hand Stella Vacarro over to my care, I'll see that she is safely escorted down to Sacramento and kept under protective custody until she can stand trial."

"No," Longarm said flatly. "Someone would ambush her. As you can see by the blood that has stained my bandanna and her dress, someone has already nearly succeeded."

"I'm the only one with enough authority to save her," Abe Huffington said. "And while I'm at it, I might as well also take those last two train robbers down to Sacramento and have them locked up for safekeeping."

"Again," Longarm said, "the answer is no."

"Use your head, Marshal! You can't possibly hold off the

entire town! I can use my influence to preserve the peace and save lives!''

''And to further your own political ambitions,'' Longarm told the man. ''That's clear enough to see.''

''Dammit!'' Abe raged. ''I just want to prevent more killing. I've lost my son and I also want justice.''

''Miss Vacarro did not kill your son,'' Longarm told the man. ''Maybe you can look a little closer to home and learn who really killed Noah.''

''It wasn't me!'' Nick screamed. ''That sonofabitch is trying to turn us against each other, Pa! You know that I loved my brother!''

''He did,'' Abe said, eyes full of pain. ''I know my boys better than anyone. Nick here is wild and he's had a few brushes with the law, but—''

''A *few*!'' Stella laughed coldly. ''Nick is the most rotten apple on your family tree! You must be wishing it was him that had been killed instead of Noah.''

''Shut up, you whore!'' Abe raged.

Longarm drove the heel of his left hand into Abe's round face, propelling the man backward so that he slammed up against the door.

''This conversation has just ended, Mr. Huffington. If you really want to see justice served, then help us get a judge and a few lawmen up here to control that mob outside. And it wouldn't hurt for someone to go around and close down the saloons. I'd do that myself but I'm occupied.''

Abe brushed his fingers across his nose to see if there was any blood. There was not.

''Marshal Long,'' he said, straightening his suit coat over his corpulent body, ''Nick and I came in here unarmed—as

102

you ordered. We tried to talk some sense into you, but it proved impossible. Now, we're going to just have to let this thing take its natural, inevitable course.''

"That sounds like a threat."

"It's no threat," Abe replied, eyes burning with hatred when he looked back at Stella. "It's a promise."

"Get out."

Abe had to help the still-dazed and probably half-drunk Nick leave the office.

"What's going to happen now?" Stella asked.

"They're going to attack as soon as it's dark," Longarm predicted. "There's little doubt in my mind about that."

"Arm us!" Jack cried. "For crissakes, Marshal, maybe together we can all stop 'em!"

"We'll stop them," Longarm promised, "but not with your brand of help."

Stella came over to stand beside Longarm. "I shouldn't have come here," she said. "I should have made a run for it."

"But you wouldn't have had any chance," Longarm said. "No chance at all."

"It will be dark in another two hours," Stella said, glancing at a window.

"In two hours," Longarm told her, "a lot of good things could happen."

"Such as?" Stella asked.

Longarm frowned, trying but unable to come up with some encouragement.

"Yeah," William said, "I have the same damned question, Marshal."

"Me too," Jack raged. "Marshal, if they get their hands on us again, we're dead men!"

"You're dead men either way," Longarm said quietly. "And there's nothing I can or even want to do to keep you from the gallows."

Chapter 10

The sun was going down and the mob was heating up when Longarm heard a loud pounding on his office door. "Who is it!"

"It's me! Marshal Walker! Open up!"

Longarm hardly recognized the voice because it was so weak. But it did sound like Marshal Walker, so he unbolted the door and peeked through the crack.

"Pete! For crying out loud! You should be in bed!"

"That's what Doc Davis kept telling me," Walker said as he pushed inside. "But you just can't keep a good lawman down, can you."

"Come on in and sit down!"

Pete staggered inside. He was weak, but a six-gun was strapped to his waist and when he collapsed on his bunk, he managed a smile. "I come to defend the fortress," he told them. "And I come to find out what the hell happened to Noah Huffington."

"I didn't see him," Longarm said. "I haven't been able to leave my prisoners for even a minute. Stella?"

"I never saw him either," she answered, "but several of

my friends did. They also saw my stiletto in his back. He'd been stabbed to death in his bedroom.''

"Was there any evidence of a struggle or of theft?'' Longarm asked.

"I don't know,'' Stella said, her voice nearly cracking. "I just heard the news and came rushing over here because I knew what awful conclusions people would immediately reach. I wanted to rush to Noah, but my friends told me that I'd be caught and maybe even hanged on the spot.''

"They might have been entirely right,'' Longarm said. "You did the smart thing.''

"Doc Davis examined the body,'' Walker said. "He told me that there were bruises all over Noah's body and face. It appeared that he'd put up one helluva good fight.''

"Those bruises could also have been inflicted by the lynch mob last night,'' Longarm said. "Noah was struck with a whiskey bottle squarely in the face and then he fell hard back into a wagon bed.''

"Yeah,'' Walker said, "we knew that, but the doctor said it was clear that he'd been in a tough fight. His knuckles were scraped up and he'd taken quite a pounding.''

"That works in our favor,'' Longarm said, "because Stella sure couldn't have beaten him that way.''

Tears began to slide down Stella's cheeks, and then she started to cry. Longarm went over to her side to comfort the poor woman. "Stella, I'm sorry, but we're just trying to put together the pieces of this puzzle.''

"I know,'' she whispered. "And there is nothing more in the world that I want than to find out who killed my poor Noah. But I shouldn't have to be hiding in jail! I should be out there trying to do something.''

"There's nothing that you can do right now,'' Longarm

told her. "Nothing except to stay alive and maybe help us solve this murder."

"I'm afraid that I'm not going to be any help with this one," Walker said. "But I can promise you that a couple of good lawmen are going to be arriving to help us put the clamp on that lynch mob. And when the dust settles, you can bet that I'm going to be making more than just a few arrests."

"If you ask me," Longarm said, "it wouldn't be such a bad idea to start with your town's mayor."

"I agree," Walker said with a yawn. "Now wake me when my friends from Placerville show up to help."

"What are their names?"

"Marshal Ed Jones and his deputy, Frank Lane," Walker answered. "They're both damned fine lawmen."

"That's good to hear."

"Stella," Walker said, "you need to have a doctor look at that bullet crease across your neck. You look like you've lost quite a lot of blood."

"I've got plenty more," Stella replied. "And anyway, he'd just want to sew it up and I'd just have to tell him no. So what's the point?"

"If that's the way you feel, then I guess you're right," Walker answered, closing his eyes.

The man fell asleep almost at once, but his arrival had a very positive effect on everyone in the room. Even the two train robbers looked much more hopeful than they had several minutes earlier.

"Maybe we do have a chance of living to see tomorrow morning," William said to his companion.

"Maybe," Jack said, "but only if more help arrives. Huffington ain't going to let any grass grow between his toes.

He left mad, and you can just bet that he and Nick are stirring up trouble out there in the street.''

Jack came over to stand near the front of the cell. He gripped the bars and said, ''If Marshal Walker's lawmen friends don't arrive in time, and if the mob gets rough, you'd better give Stella to 'em, Marshal Long. You do that, might be they'll leave us be.''

''You're just one hell of a conniving sonofabitch, aren't you, Jack. Always looking for the quick and easy way out no matter who gets hurt.''

''Hell, yes, I am!'' Jack angrily shouted. ''And I suppose you wouldn't be if you were looking to be hanged!''

Longarm didn't even bother to answer. He divided up the basket of food that Lola had brought for them, and everyone ate in silence, listening to the noise out in the street. They heard both Abe and Nick Huffington's strident voices, and knew that the pair were inciting the crowd to rush the marshal's office and take the law into their own hands for the second night in a row. ''I sure hope that Pete's lawmen friends from Placerville get here soon,'' Longarm said. ''If we have enough bodies to make a good show of force, I believe we can bluff down that mob. But if it's just the three of us . . . well, it might come down to blood and bullets.''

''Yeah,'' Stella said, coming over to wrap her arms around his neck and hug him tightly. ''This is turning into a nightmare! I'm sorry that I dragged you into it, Custis.''

''Don't be sorry about that,'' Longarm told her. ''I've had an . . . an interesting time already, and the worst thing in the world for me is boredom. Believe me, I haven't been bored since my train was robbed.''

Stella managed a smile. ''Do you think that you can find out who really killed Noah?''

"I'm sure going to try," he said, "but I need to examine the body and the room where he was killed. Then I need to start asking questions and poking around for clues. My hunch is that Noah might have been killed by some friend of Abe Huffington determined that Noah not marry you and create a scandal that could jeopardize Abe's political future."

"I was thinking that might be the motive," Stella said. "But there are probably dozens of people who would stand to lose a great deal if Abe isn't elected the new governor of California. So even if that were the motive, I still don't see how you could narrow it down."

"Well," Longarm mused, "sometimes these things just have a way of working themselves out to a logical conclusion. But it all takes time to investigate. And time, Stella, is something that you might not have."

"What do you mean?"

"I mean that if we get a hanging judge who just wants to get this whole business taken care of in a big hurry, it could be very bad for you, Stella."

"Then what—"

"I don't know," Longarm interrupted. "We'll just have to wait and see how the cards fall. But I won't stand by and let this town's lynching fever sweep you away. That much I promise."

"I should have just run," Stella said. "That would have been best for everyone."

"We've already gone over the reasons why you couldn't do that," Longarm told her. "In the eyes of most people, running would be an admission of guilt."

"I suppose it would," she replied, "but—"

Stella's words were cut short by a loud knock at the door. "Marshal Walker, it's Ed Jones and Frank Lane! Open up!"

"It's them," Longarm said, moving quickly to open the door and greet their reinforcements.

Jones took one quick look around and sized up the grim situation. After introductions were made, Jones went over to his old friend and awakened him. "Pete, you have a pretty big crowd gathering out there. Why don't you just lay back down and let us handle it."

"Not on your life," Walker growled. "You and Frank sure took your time getting here."

"There's more help on the way too," Lane promised. "We've got people riding in from Yuba City in Nevada."

"Is that a fact!" Walker said, grinning.

"It sure is," Jones replied. "We all got to stick together in times of trouble. Ain't that right?"

"Yep," Walker said. "Marshal Custis Long here is a *federal* officer, but I don't want you boys to hold that entirely against him."

"We won't," Jones replied.

"Pleased to meet you," Deputy Lane said. "I wish us local authorities made the money you Feds make."

"Well," Longarm said, "I sincerely doubt that any of us are in this line of work with the expectation of getting rich. Now, I'm going to bow to you local lawmen, so how should we handle that mob outside—or do you think we ought to just wait them out until we get even more help?"

"I don't think we have that much time," Jones said. "They wouldn't even have let us in here if they'd been halfway sober and realized what we were up to. The trouble is quickly coming to a head."

"Then let's step outside and take charge," Longarm suggested.

"Sounds like a good idea to me," Deputy Lane, a fresh-faced youth in his early twenties, replied.

"Now wait a damned minute!" Jack shouted from the cell. "What if you heroes go out there and get gunned down! There's a big damned bunch of hard-drinking and angry folks outside. Marshal Long, you may have forgotten what they did to our friends last night in your city park, but I damn sure haven't!"

"And neither have I," Longarm said. "But there was only one lawman standing against all of them last night. Now, there's four."

"Five," Stella reminded him as she raised her shotgun overhead. "I'll be right behind you."

"Who is *she*?" Deputy Lane asked, staring.

"Long story," Longarm answered, "and one that will have to wait until later. Let's get those men outside under control and then we can all sit down and sort things out."

"Let's do it!" Jones said, drawing his six-gun.

Longarm waited until Marshal Walker was on his feet and moving toward the door with his gun in his fist. Then he stepped out in front of the others with the shotgun and kicked the door open so hard it slammed against the wall.

If some drunken fool opened fire out there, a lot of men were going to go down with him.

Chapter 11

When Longarm, Marshal Walker, and the two lawmen from Placerville opened the door and stepped outside, the crowd fell silent. Longarm waited for Walker to speak, but when he glanced sideways at the man, he knew that it was all the wounded marshal could do just to remain on his feet and that he simply lacked the strength to confront the lynch mob.

"Marshal Long, we want all three of them!" Abe Huffington shouted.

The crowd roared in agreement. Nick Huffington stepped out from the others. "You know that Stella Vacarro murdered my brother, so hand her over! We ain't afraid to hang a woman same as a man!"

The crowd roared again, and Longarm knew they were working themselves up to attack in force. "Either disperse right now, or I'm putting you all under arrest!" he bellowed, raising his shotgun and pointing it at the lynch mob.

Beside him, the three other lawmen did the same with their pistols, and it must have been pretty intimidating to see four weapons leveled at them because the angry crowd couldn't retreat fast enough.

"I'm getting a judge here tomorrow!" Abe Huffington blustered. "We'll have a trial and a verdict this week and *then* we'll hang them all!"

"We'll see about that," Longarm replied as the crowd began to filter back into the saloons.

"That was close," Deputy Lane said, expelling a deep sigh of relief. "Marshal Long?"

"Yeah?"

"Would you really have opened fire?"

"Damn right he would have!" Walker wheezed. "We *all* would have to protect our prisoners."

"We were sworn to uphold the law," Longarm said. "I just wouldn't have had any choice, no matter how much I hated to pull the trigger."

"Yeah," Lane said, "I guess you're right."

"Being a lawman sometimes calls for some very difficult choices," Longarm said as he followed the others back inside and closed the door.

He could see that Walker was ready to collapse, so he helped the older man over to his bunk. "Pete, I'm going to send for the doctor."

"No point in that. He's already done everything he can to patch me up. I'm on the mend and I ain't going anywhere until this trouble is over."

"What if they pay some damned judge to sentence us all to hang!" Jack shouted from inside his jail cell. "They could bribe a judge, couldn't they? And then what kind of justice would that be?"

"You're both going to hang anyway," Marshal Walker wheezed. "It's Stella that we're worried about, not you two rotten sonofabitches."

Now that the question had been raised, Longarm wanted

114

to pursue it a little further. After filling in Marshal Jones and Deputy Lane about the murder of Noah Huffington and the accusation against Stella, Longarm turned back to Walker. "Pete, could they find a crooked judge in this county?" he asked.

"I'm afraid that old Judge Gross would take a bribe," Pete Walker admitted as he looked to his friends from Placerville. "Ed, what do you think?"

The marshal from Placerville nodded. "Judge Gross has fallen on hard times in his old age. He drinks too much and I hear he's in rough financial as well as physical shape. There's no doubt in my mind he'd take a bribe, if it'd keep him in whiskey for a few weeks."

"I'll bet you anything that's who they've gone for," Walker said. "I hear that Judge Gross is living in some run-down shack down in Coloma. When he's sober, which isn't very often, he's trying to scratch out a dime novel about being a hanging judge during the Forty-Niner gold rush."

"How far is Coloma from here?" Longarm asked.

"Ten, fifteen miles at the most," Walker replied. "They could go fetch the judge and have him back and in a courtroom as early as tomorrow afternoon."

"He'd hang his mother for a bottle of whiskey," Deputy Lane said. "They say he's hanged more than forty men and has always wanted to hang a woman."

Longarm went over to Stella, who had turned pale. "Listen," he said, "I know that you didn't kill Noah and I'm not going to let some besotted old judge send you to the gallows."

"It sounds to me like there's not going to be anything you can do," Stella replied. "If the man is still a judge in the state of California, he can hold court and come to a swift hanging verdict.''

"Not if he can't find you,'' Longarm answered. ''I think the only solution is to hide you someplace safe until I can find out who took your stiletto and really murdered Noah. We just need some time.''

"I agree,'' Walker said. ''Because if Judge Gross shows up tomorrow, he'd have a guilty verdict the next day.''

"Then that's what we'll do,'' Longarm decided, going over to the window and staring out into the dark street. ''We'll sneak out just as soon as the street is clear.''

"You could take her over to Placerville and hide her there,'' Deputy Lane suggested. ''Marshal Jones and I have a lot of friends who would help you out.''

But Longarm shook his head. ''No, we'll find someplace for her to hide that is much closer.''

Stella nodded. ''I have a good, safe place in mind.''

"When the Huffingtons find out she's gone, they'll go crazy,'' Walker warned.

"Let them,'' Longarm testily replied. ''You can tell them that Deputy Lane took her to . . . to Sacramento.''

"Me?'' Lane asked with surprise. ''Take a prisoner to Sacramento?''

"You'll just be a decoy,'' Longarm explained to the young lawman.

"He's making sense, Frank,'' Marshal Jones said. ''You just ride on over to Sacramento. Put up in a hotel and then the next day sneak out and return to keep the lid on things back in Placerville. By the time this Huffington crowd realizes they've been tricked, Marshal Long can have Noah's *real* murderer locked up in this jail.''

"All right," the young deputy agreed. "Then I guess we'll all three leave together?"

"That's the plan," Longarm told him.

"Hey!" Jack shouted from his jail cell. "Why don't the deputy take us with him to Sacramento where we can get a fair trial? We won't get one here!"

"You'll have a court trial," Longarm told the prisoner. "But since you're both guilty, it doesn't make a damn bit of difference where you're hanged—just as long as you both *are* hanged!"

Jack cursed a blue streak at them, but the older prisoner named William just sat on his bunk with his head held low, staring blankly at the floor.

After that, they all waited until after midnight when the street was empty. Then Longarm put a coat and Stetson on Stella and led her to the front door saying, "We're going to need some horses."

"I've got a friend with a corral full," Stella replied. "We can trust him to keep a secret."

"Good," Longarm answered. "Just keep your head low and lead the way. I'll make sure we are not being followed."

"I've got my own horse," Deputy Lane said, extending his hand. "Good luck, Custis. I just wish that I could stay and help out here in Auburn."

"You can help us most by being a decoy," Longarm said. "And by getting back to Placerville and maintaining the law."

"Yeah, I suppose," Lane said, but he still looked disappointed.

Longarm nodded to his friend Pete. "You just take care of yourself."

"Oh, sure," Pete said. "I expect that I'll be hearing from you in a day or two."

"You will," Longarm promised as he pushed outside followed by Stella.

"Just follow me," she whispered.

As soon as they reached the end of the first block, Stella turned right and then ducked into an alley. If there had not been a full moon, Longarm was sure that they would have been in trouble as they made their way down the dark, litter-strewn alley in what was definitely not one of Auburn's nicer sections. Several times, dogs began to bark loudly, and one almost charged out and attacked them, but Longarm grabbed a board and the animal slunk away.

"How far is this place?" Longarm asked.

"Just up ahead," Stella assured him.

Ten minutes later they were almost to the outskirts of town when Stella halted and then pointed to a run-down shack with a nearby horse corral.

"It belongs to old Julio Ortiz," she told Longarm. "He is a very close friend."

"Will Julio realize that he'll be taking a risk by helping us?"

"He won't care," Stella assured him. "Julio lives alone. I hire him to do odd jobs at my saloon, and I've been able to do little favors for him for a number of years. He's a very good man and was a *vaquero* until he became too stiff to risk any more bad falls from a horse. Now, he trains them mostly on the ground, and I often loan him money to buy broncs and outlaw horses that he can tame and then resell at a good profit."

"Then lead the way," Longarm said as they crept forward toward the shack.

As soon as Stella knocked, a dog inside began to bark. Longarm heard the distinctly metallic *click* of a gun being cocked, then a soft "Who is it?"

"It's Stella. I am with Marshal Long. We need to borrow some horses, Julio."

They heard the old California *vaquero* quiet his barking dog before he opened the door and stood silhouetted in lamplight.

"Señorita Vacarro! I heard about Señor Huffington being killed. I am so sorry!"

"So am I," Stella replied sadly. "Julio, this is a good friend, Marshal Custis Long. He is also helping me. We need horses and a place to hide."

"You could stay here."

"No," Stella said. "They would think to come and search this place and you might become a target for their anger."

"I am not afraid to die for someone like you," Julio vowed, straightening up and puffing out his chest like a fearless old fighting rooster.

Longarm was impressed. Although Julio Ortiz was bent and could not have weighed over 125 pounds soaking wet, he had courage and dignity.

"We need two good horses," Longarm explained. "It would help if they had speed and endurance."

"Of course, Señor," Ortiz said. "Would you both care to come inside?"

"Thank you, but no," Stella replied. "We'll wait by the corral for you."

"I have two very fine horses for you, Señorita," Ortiz promised them.

"Thank you."

Longarm and Stella walked over to the corral. There were

about twenty horses penned up inside, but half of them were lying down and the rest were bunched up together, so that it was impossible to judge their quality.

"I know a very good place to hide," Stella said. "It's only about six miles to the east, but higher up in the hills. It used to be an old prospector's cabin and I bought it from him a few years ago when he was destitute."

"That sounds good to me," Longarm said. "But what about food for ourselves and the horses?"

"I keep the place stocked. It was a hideaway for Noah and me. We . . ." Stella's voice cracked with emotion. "We spent a lot of happy times there."

"I'm sorry that—"

But Stella didn't let him finish because she placed her finger against his lips. "Noah wouldn't want me to grieve," she said. "And so I won't."

Julio emerged into the moonlight with a braided leather reata. He entered the corral, the reata dangling loosely from his right hand. The horses began to mill about with agitation, and Longarm saw the reata snake out to catch a tall buckskin gelding. The animal froze, and Julio soon had it bridled and was leading it outside the corral.

"This one is for you, Señor," he said with obvious pride. "A fine animal, no?"

"Very fine," Longarm agreed.

"Now yours, Señorita," Julio said as he re-entered the corral and quickly roped a beautiful sorrel mare.

They had both animals saddled ten minutes later, and Julio gave them a bag full of tortillas and a jug of strong red wine. "This is to keep you warm tonight," he said with a slight bow. "Adios!"

"I won't soon forget this, Julio. And if anyone comes asking if you have seen me . . ."

"My lips will forever be sealed," he vowed.

They rode swiftly away, and the horses were eager to run. Since both Longarm and Stella were wearing coats with their hats pulled down low, Longarm knew that neither one of them would have been recognized, even if they had come upon some night travelers. The six or seven miles they traveled took them at least another couple of thousand feet higher, and the air grew cold, while the stars seemed to glitter even more intensely.

Stella's little cabin was set deep in the forest beside a fine stream. There was a corral hidden behind the cabin for the horses, and grass hay in a lean-to barn where they stored their saddles, bridles, and blankets.

Stella lit a candle, and Longarm could see that the inside of her cabin had been completely refurbished. It had a good hardwood floor, comfortable furniture, and a very well-stocked pantry.

"I should probably light a fire," Longarm said, briskly rubbing his hands together. "But I'm worried that someone would see the smoke and come to investigate."

"I know," she replied. "Noah and I always had the same worry."

"So what did you do?"

"We went to bed and pulled the comforter over us to keep warm," Stella told him.

Longarm didn't know what to say about that, and he must have looked a bit uncomfortable because Stella laughed and took his hand saying, "We've made love before. Why are you acting so bashful?"

"Because you are engaged."

121

"Noah is gone," she told him, "and it's freezing in here. So let's go to bed and get warmed up. We don't have to do anything but sleep."

"I could never just sleep in bed with you," Longarm confessed.

"Well," Stella said, "I'll just have to take my chances then, won't I."

The bed was cold and they were both shivering as they crawled under the covers. Longarm wrapped his arms around Stella and tried to stop shivering. Her breath was warm on his face, and the smell of her hair brought passionate memories rushing back so strongly that Longarm felt himself becoming aroused. And as if that wasn't bad enough, Stella began to kiss his face and nuzzle his neck.

"Stella, are you sure this is such a good idea?" he asked, feeling his manhood throbbing and straining to escape his pants.

"I don't know," she whispered, unbuttoning her blouse.

Longarm didn't know either. But Stella was big-breasted and warm and he wanted her. Longarm unbuttoned his own shirt, and then he kissed Stella hard. Her tongue entered his mouth and the next thing he knew, she was jumping out of bed and undressing.

"Hurry up, darling!" she pleaded.

Longarm had run completely out of reasons why making love to Stella was wrong. He rolled out of bed, kicked off his boots, and then unbuckled his gun belt and placed it on the chair next to the bed. Shucking out of his pants but not bothering to remove his socks, he leaped back under the covers.

Stella was waiting. She took his big root in her hand and guided it up between her legs.

"I didn't think we'd ever be like this again," she breathed. "Custis, I loved Noah Huffington, but he couldn't excite or satisfy me the way you always could."

"Stella, don't talk so damned much," Longarm said, pushing deeper into her voluptuous body until their union grew slick and then hot.

Stella liked it deep and hard, and Longarm was more than happy to oblige her. Soon the woman was bucking and moaning under his weight, and Longarm lost himself in their lovemaking. Time stopped and they went on and on until they were both perspiring heavily and panting hard.

"Here I go!" she finally cried, thrusting upward and gripping him with all her might.

Longarm was ready too. He plunged up and down until he had finally extinguished the hot, sweet fire in his loins.

Stella went limp underneath him, and he felt tears on her cheeks.

"Why are you crying? Is it for Noah?"

"No," she said, "it's because I haven't lost the capacity for loving. After I learned that Noah had been murdered, I was very afraid that I would."

"It's all going to work out," Longarm promised. "I'll find out who murdered Noah and bring him to justice."

"I know," she said, "but even after that, I need to get away from Auburn. Sell everything and start over again."

"Where would you go?"

"I was thinking of Denver."

Longarm was glad that there was just a candle burning. He wasn't sure whether to be glad or worried about Stella coming to Denver. After all, she was a damned irresistible woman, and he had no doubt that he had something to do with her choice for a relocation.

Stella reached down and stroked him. "What do you think about that?" she asked. "Would you like me for a neighbor . . . or roommate?"

"I would," he said, because it was the truth. "But there is a little problem."

"And what might that be?"

"If we weren't careful," he said, "we might just spend all our time together in bed and get little else done."

Stella laughed and then kissed him again. "You know what I was thinking?"

"No."

"I was thinking that I would be dangling from a rope if you hadn't come to attend my wedding."

"That's a pretty grim thing to be thinking," he said. "Can't you come up with something more pleasant?"

Stella's hand tightened around his manhood, coaxing it to rise like the head of a big cobra. "I can think of a *lot* of more pleasant things right now, Custis. In fact, I'm going to show you a few of them."

When Stella began to slide down his body, lips playing across his flesh, Longarm groaned with pleasure because he knew exactly what she had in mind.

Chapter 12

It was almost noon when Longarm finally opened his eyes after a long night of lovemaking. He rolled over to watch Stella for a few minutes, and wondered if he could live with her in Denver. He hadn't roomed with anyone in a long, long time, and had grown so fixed in his daily habits that he was not completely sure he could adapt to living with anyone. Stella was beautiful, loving, generous, and passionate, but she was also stubborn and very strong-willed. She'd either want to rearrange his place, or get a bigger and fancier house, probably much like the one that she had bought in Auburn. More possessions meant more worries and less independence. Longarm wasn't entirely sure that he wanted to change that much.

But Stella was an extraordinary woman, tough, resourceful, and very intelligent. She was a scrapper, which Longarm considered to be a major attribute in both men and women. He especially admired a woman with both beauty and strength, and doubted that he'd ever find that combination in greater evidence than in Stella.

Well, he decided, there was no reason to worry about what

might not happen. By now all of Auburn would realize that Stella had been spirited out of their jail. Hopefully, everyone would think that the deputy had escorted her to Sacramento. That being the case, Longarm figured he would show up in town and begin his murder investigation. If someone challenged him about Stella's real whereabouts, he would just claim ignorance.

Longarm slipped out of bed and gathered his clothes. The cabin had warmed a little, but it was still very chilly inside. He tiptoed over to the door and dressed quickly before he buckled on his gun belt and carried his boots outside. Sitting in the sunlight, he pulled on his socks and then his boots, then stood up and stretched. He felt pretty wrung out after last night's long and passionate lovemaking, but that didn't keep him from smiling as he watched a squirrel nibble on a pinecone while loudly scolding him.

Longarm went around behind the corral and forked some of the grass hay to the horses. He would give the buckskin an hour to eat its fill, and then he was going to ride on back down to Auburn and investigate Noah Huffington's untimely death. He'd visit the undertaker and examine the body, then go to Noah's house and poke around looking for evidence. If Noah had put up as good a fight as his knuckles indicated, his assassin might have some serious facial bruises, maybe a black eye or a split lip. Of course, that by itself wouldn't be enough evidence to arrest a man, but it would at least be a starting point in his investigation.

"Good morning!" Stella said when he went back into the cabin.

"Good morning," he replied. "I wish I could cook you some breakfast and pour us both a cup of coffee, but that could be a problem."

"I suppose," she replied. "Noah and I always made just a *little* fire in the stove, one that hardly gave off any smoke. Noah and I had to get out of bed to cook and eat once in a while. Besides, I can't hide up here and go hungry while you poke around Auburn."

"No," Longarm agreed, "I suppose not. All right, I'll get the stove fired up and you can do the cooking."

He had to go outside and chop firewood, but that posed no problem, and once they had a fire going, Stella was all business. They soon enjoyed coffee and a big stack of pancakes, which they doused liberally with maple syrup.

"I have to get going," Longarm said when he'd had his fill.

"You'll be back tonight, won't you?"

"Yes. Don't worry, but it might be late. I mean to stick around until I've made some kind of progress. Any suspects that I ought to start with?"

Stella frowned. "The most likely suspect is Noah's brother, Nick."

"He's already at the top of my list," Longarm said. "Anyone else?"

"His father?"

"No," Longarm said, "I don't think so. Abe Huffington may be a crooked and ruthless politician, but he did love his son and I really can't imagine him killing Noah."

"You're right," Stella said. "Abe hates my guts, but he did love his favorite son."

"Is there anyone besides Noah's brother that stands to profit from his murder?"

"Not that I can think of," Stella said. "Abe is pretty wealthy and Nick is very greedy, so that seems to be a pretty good motive to me."

127

"And also to me," Longarm said. "It's also entirely possible that Nick got his hands on your stiletto, then hired someone to use it to murder Noah. That way, he would have an airtight alibi when Noah was killed."

"Well, then how would you ever get a conviction?"

"Somehow," Longarm said, "I'd have to get the real killer to confess that he'd been hired by Noah. He might, for example, do this in exchange for a prison sentence instead of a death sentence."

"I see."

"Does Nick know anyone who would do such a thing?"

"Lots of people," Stella answered. "He runs with a pretty rough crowd over in Placerville. There's one man named Art Mead who is a known gun for hire. He's a tall, thin man with a horrible knife scar across the right side of his face. I wouldn't be surprised if he's been hired by Nick before."

"I'll check him out," Longarm promised.

When Longarm rode back into Auburn, he went straight to the marshal's office, and learned that both Abe and Nick Huffington had been extremely upset to learn that Stella was missing.

"What did you tell them?" Longarm asked.

Marshal Walker shrugged. "I said that we figured justice would be better served in Sacramento. Now, I didn't actually *say* that that was where you or the deputy took Stella, but that's sure enough the conclusion that the Huffingtons reached. I understand that they boarded today's noon train that will take them down to Sacramento."

"Good," Longarm said. "With Abe and his son out of the way, I can operate a little more freely in this investigation."

128

"Where are you going to start?"

"With the undertaker, I suppose."

"He's kind of strange," Walker cautioned. "It would probably help if I went along with you."

"Are you up to that?" Longarm said, worried that the man was still weak and unsteady.

"Yeah," Walker replied. "I won't be none too fast getting over there, and my head is still throbbing like a Comanche's war drum, but I'll make it. Fact is, some fresh air might perk me up a bit."

"Suit yourself," Longarm told him. "But there may be some folks out there that will want to cause you some grief."

"I know that," Walker replied, "and that's why I'd like to have you along."

Longarm understood completely. Marshal Walker needed his support in case some hothead did want to make a fight.

"Then let's go," Longarm said, opening the door.

"You men be careful," Marshal Jones warned.

"Count on it," Longarm told the lawman from Placerville as he walked outside.

The very first person they met was Lola, who came hurrying up to greet them. "Pete," she said, taking the marshal's arm, "you shouldn't be up and around so soon."

"Ah," the marshal answered, "I'll be fine. I just need some fresh air and exercise."

"You need *rest*," Lola argued, taking his arm as they walked down the boardwalk.

When they reached the undertaker's office and went inside, Longarm could smell the mixture of formaldehyde and death. A short, nervous man appeared wearing a black coat, starched white shirt, and black tie.

"My, my," he said, eyes darting between his visitors. "It

is good to see you up and about, Marshal Walker! But I really didn't expect any visitors."

"We want to examine Noah Huffington's body," Walker told the man.

"I'm afraid that won't be possible."

"Why not?"

"Mr. Huffington collected his son's body and it accompanied him to Sacramento."

"Are you sure?" Longarm asked.

"Of course I'm sure," the undertaker replied. "Believe me, I had expected to handle all the arrangements and that the deceased would be buried right here in Auburn. But then, without even the courtesy of a warning, Mr. Huffington and his son appeared this morning and told me to place the body in my best coffin and that they would transport it to Sacramento. I was very, very upset, but what could I do?"

"Nothing, I suppose," Longarm said, wondering if it would be worth traveling to Sacramento.

"What can you tell us about Noah's wounds?" Walker asked the undertaker.

"They were dreadful . . . and fatal, of course."

Longarm frowned. "How many times did it appear that he was actually stabbed?"

"At least five. All in the back."

"*All* in the back?"

"That's right," the mortician replied. "Why do you sound surprised?"

"Because," Longarm said, "we understand that Noah's knuckles were bruised and it was obvious that he had put up a hard struggle before being murdered."

"The part about his knuckles is true," the undertaker said. "And poor Mr. Huffington did suffer a terrible beating."

130

"How do you explain that?" Longarm asked. "I mean, if Noah had been caught by surprise and stabbed repeatedly in the back, how could he have had the strength to fight his murderer?"

"I haven't any idea," the undertaker answered. "And frankly, that kind of question is not one that I choose to ponder. My job is to insure the dignity of the deceased, not try to guess how or why they died."

"Who has the stiletto?" Longarm asked, looking to both men for the answer.

"I don't know," Walker admitted, looking a little sheepish. "Maybe Dr. Davis."

"I'll talk to him," Longarm said. "Has anyone seen Judge Gross yet?"

"I heard that he's arrived," Walker said. "And that a jury is already being selected to sentence and then hang those last two train robbers."

Longarm nodded with understanding, and was glad that Stella wasn't also going to be the victim of Judge Gross's kangaroo court. "Well," he mused, "I guess that there is no point in hanging around here now that we know Noah's body has been removed."

"I overheard Mr. Huffington say that Noah would be buried tomorrow morning."

"We could get to Sacramento in time to examine the body," Walker suggested.

"No," Longarm said, "that won't be necessary."

"Then what are we going to do now?"

"*You* are going to go back to bed," Longarm replied. "Lola, why don't you take him home and then chain him to his bed, if you have to."

"I will," she replied, taking the marshal's arm and heading outside.

"One more question," Longarm said before leaving the undertaker. "To the best of your recollection, did you see anything unusual about the body?"

"Such as?"

"I don't know. A bullet wound or evidence of poisoning?"

"No. Most definitely not," the man said without hesitation, "but why don't you ask Dr. Davis?"

"I will," Longarm promised, heading outside, "but I doubt that he gave the man a thorough examination given all that has gone on in this town and that his main concern was caring for Marshal Walker."

Longarm was about to say more when he heard a rifle shot. His hand reached for his gun and he was out the door just in time to see Lola collapsing beside Marshal Walker, who was lying in the street. Out of the corner of his eye Longarm saw a flash of movement, and looked up to see a rifleman on the roof of the mercantile building. The man fired again and Walker's body convulsed as it took the impact of a second bullet.

Longarm opened fire, hoping to wound the rifleman. But his very first bullet struck the man in the chest and his second slug spun him halfway around, causing the ambusher to pitch forward and do a complete somersault before his body slammed down on the boardwalk. It wasn't necessary for Longarm to go examine the body because he knew that the ambusher was dead.

"Pete!"

Walker was gone. Lola threw her arms around Longarm's

neck and hugged him tightly. "Why!" she wailed. "Why did they have to murder him!"

"I don't know."

"He was such a nice man!"

"Yes," Longarm replied, "and also a damned fine lawman."

Marshal Jones appeared, gun in hand. He took one look at Pete's bullet-riddled body and said, "Dammit, what the hell is going on in this town!"

"I can't answer that either," Longarm said, "but one way or another, I swear that we'll find out."

Chapter 13

Longarm took control of the situation. "Everyone listen up!" he shouted, marching over to the dead ambusher. "This man has just shot down Marshal Walker. Who is he!"

The gathering crowd gawked at the two dead men, but said nothing.

"I asked you to identify this cold-blooded ambusher!" Longarm angrily bellowed. "Is anyone man enough to step forward and help?"

An old, gray-bearded fellow in baggy overalls detached himself from the crowd. "His name was Claude Blanton."

Longarm hurried over to the man. "Where does he live?"

"Down the railroad line somewhere around Newcastle," the informant replied. "He rode over here once in a while to trade a horse or raise a little hell. Blanton was a bad one."

"Who did he work for?"

"I dunno," the old man replied, shaking his head. "He ran with a tough bunch. Seemed to me that they did a little of everything outside the law including claim jumping and horse stealing. Once in a while, he'd get a job drivin' freight wagons for the Central Pacific, and I hear he was a good mule skinner. But he never stuck at anything very long.''

"Thanks," Longarm said. "What's your name?"

"Fred Potts. I own a little harness repair shop just up the street. I liked Marshal Walker. We were friends for a lot of years. Damn shame that a fine man like him was ambushed by a snake like Claude Blanton.''

"I agree," Longarm said bitterly. He looked around at the others in the crowd. "Anyone else have anything to say about Blanton?''

"I was in the Rusty Bucket Saloon last night where Blanton was drinking pretty hard," another man offered.

"So was I," a smallish fellow with bloodshot blue eyes and a crumpled hat added.

"Yeah, I saw him there too," Potts said.

"Anyone else see Blanton in the last couple of days?"

Several men raised their hands.

"All right then," Longarm said. "I'd need to have a few words with all of you as soon as we get things taken care of here. We'll meet at the marshal's office.''

Longarm started to turn away, then hesitated. "I'd like to say one last thing. You folks had one of the best marshals I've ever known, and you treated him badly even though he was just trying to carry out the law. This town didn't *deserve* a man like Pete Walker. But now that you've lost him, at least a few of you are trying to set things right by telling me what you know about his murderer.''

Longarm went over and gently pulled Lola to her feet. The young woman was very upset and tears were coursing down her cheeks.

"We're all going to miss him," Longarm said. "It's just a damn rotten shame.''

Lola nodded and leaned against Longarm's chest. He

136

looked over to Marshal Jones. "Will you take care of things here?"

"Sure," Jones said, "we'll get the bodies to the undertaker's office and I'll get the names of everyone who spoke up about seeing Blanton."

"Thanks," Longarm told the lawman. Then he led Lola away asking, "Where are you staying?"

"At the Central Hotel," she replied. "It's just up the street and over a block."

Longarm escorted Lola to her hotel room. It hurt him to see how hard she was taking Walker's death. "I wish I could say something that would help," Longarm said as he stood awkwardly beside her door. "There's just nothing fair about life, and I don't have any idea why Blanton killed Pete. But after I interview those people who stepped forward, I'll be going down to Newcastle to find out who might have hired him."

"What if he *wasn't* hired?" Lola asked. "What if Claude Blanton just had an old grudge against Pete, got drunk, and then decided to ambush him?"

"That's always a possibility," Longarm admitted, "but not too likely. My guess is that Blanton was hired to ambush Pete. Maybe he was even hoping to put a bullet in me before he turned and ran. Lola, I just don't know yet—but I won't rest until I find out."

She wiped tears from her face. "Do you know what Pete asked the last time we were alone together?"

"No."

"He asked me to marry him. Can you imagine? He said he was probably old enough to be my father and that he wasn't the man he'd once been, but he said he would make me happy. I believed that, Custis. I agreed to marry him. We were going to go away and live quietly. I was going to . . . to change. Honest to God, I really was!"

"I believe you."

"Why! Why did this have to happen!"

"I don't know," Longarm replied. "Good people often die much too young. At least Pete had a reasonably long life. And for what it's worth, I think you'll find someone else who can also make you happy."

She wiped her eyes dry and took a few hesitant steps forward. "I'd quickly gotten used to the idea of marrying a lawman. Maybe sometime, we . . ."

"I'll be around," Longarm said quickly as he closed her door behind him.

He wasted no time returning to the marshal's office, and was relieved to see that everyone who had stepped forward out in the street, plus at least a half dozen more, were waiting outside to help with the investigation.

"I thank you all for coming," he told them. "This town meant a lot to Pete, and now I am finally starting to understand why. And don't worry, I'm going to talk to each of you individually and in strict confidence."

"We ain't afraid of nothing happening if we talk," a man said. "Blanton was a hardcase and a troublemaker. We don't want that kind coming into Auburn and gunning our people down. If he was working with others, we want them brought to justice. Right now, none of us are feeling too proud about the things that have been going on in Auburn."

"Good," Longarm said, looking to the old harness maker. "You volunteered first, so you can be the first to come inside and tell me whatever you know."

Fred Potts nodded, spat tobacco juice on the boardwalk, and followed Longarm inside.

"Have a seat," Longarm told him, motioning toward Pete's old desk chair.

"Uh-uh," Potts said. "I wouldn't think of sitting in a dead man's chair. Be terrible luck."

"Then sit in Deputy Quaid's. I guess you would consider that to also be bad luck."

"Yep. You want to sit, fine. I'll stand."

"Fair enough," Longarm said, taking the marshal's chair. "Just begin at the beginning. Tell me everything you know about Claude Blanton."

"I've known the ornery sonofabitch since he was a shaver. His father was gunned down about ten years ago trying to hold up a stagecoach. Claude was probably there, but no one could prove it. The kid was as bad as his pa and a crack shot, when he was sober."

Longarm leaned forward intently in the office chair. "Mr. Potts, as far as you know, did Claude have any reason to hate Marshal Walker enough to kill him?"

"That's real hard to say," the old man replied, spitting on the floor and then opening a tin of chewing tobacco and stuffing it into the corner of his mouth where his beard was stained the most.

He chewed a minute, then continued. "You see, Pete had to throw Claude in jail a bunch of times. Why, he even had to pistol-whip him once or twice. There was no love lost between them."

"But was there enough hate to ambush the man in broad daylight?"

Potts scowled. "When Claude was drinking, he got real crazy. So I'd have to say that, yes, he was the kind that might do such a thing no matter what the risks or the hour."

139

"Was Blanton drinking with friends last night in the Rusty Bucket Saloon?"

"He had no friends. At least, not unless they were buying the drinks. But after their money was gone, so was he."

"Did you see anybody buying him drinks last night?"

"Yep."

"Who?"

"Another entirely ornery sonofabitch. A fella by the name of Art Mead."

Longarm sat up straight. "And he'd be from Placerville. Right?"

"How'd you guess?"

"Well," Longarm answered, "it's just that a few pieces might finally be starting to fall together. Art Mead, as I understand it, is a good friend of Nick Huffington."

"That's right," Potts said. The old man folded his arms across his skinny chest. "Are you thinking that Nick hired Art, who then got Claude drunk enough to ambush the marshal?"

"I think that is a fair possibility," Longarm answered. "But I've no proof to back it up and I doubt that Mead is going to want to talk."

"He's a real sidewinder," Potts cautioned. "You find him, you better be ready for anything. The man wears a hideout derringer up his sleeve, but he's mighty fast with his six-gun. He and Nick used to spend weeks at a time practicing the draw-and-shoot down by the old lumber mill just east of town. We could hear them from morning to night. They're each as good a gunny as you'll likely ever come across."

"Thanks for the warning," Longarm said. "Have you got any idea where I can find Art Mead?"

"Nope. But I expect he won't be hard to track down. Man

has a big scar on a face that isn't easy to forget."

"Anything else you can tell me?" Longarm said, coming to his feet.

"Afraid not. I'm just damn glad that you plugged Blanton and we don't have to worry about hanging the sonofabitch. He was a killer and a snake, that's for certain. I don't know how many men he might have backshot in the past, but I'll bet it was more than a few. You did the town a service by drilling him through the gizzard, Marshal."

"I was hoping to just wound the man so that I could get some answers from him, but there wasn't time to take a more careful aim." Longarm stuck out his hand. "Thanks, Fred. I really appreciate your being the first man to have the guts to step forward."

"You're welcome. Maybe one of the others outside can give you something else to go on. But if you ask me, the blood trail will probably pass through Art Mead straight to Nick Huffington and his father. They all crawled out of the same rotten bed of worms."

After Potts, Longarm carefully interviewed each of the other town members hoping to establish an even stronger link between Blanton, Mead, and Nick Huffington. And while several other witnesses confirmed seeing Mead buying Blanton drinks, no one saw or overheard anything that Longarm could use as evidence of a murder conspiracy. Still, their stories were consistent enough to make Longarm think that he was on the right track.

"Has anyone seen Mead in town today?" he asked the last man he interviewed.

"Art Mead rode out of town late last night. He was pretty drunk and heading back to Placerville."

"Thanks."

Longarm waited until Marshal Jones returned to the office after making funeral arrangements. When he told Jones of his plan to go to Placerville, the lawman said, "I should have sent Art Mead either to the undertaker or to prison years ago, but he's slick and I just never thought that I had a solid case. Besides that, he's Nick's friend and I knew that the Huffingtons would hire a real good lawyer."

"Well," Longarm said, "we don't have a case against the man either. But maybe I can rattle him into saying something that will tip his hand."

"Don't count on that," the lawman solemnly warned. "And don't turn your back on the man or you'll wind up just as dead as poor old Pete."

"So I hear."

"Mead carries a derringer up his sleeve."

"I know," Longarm replied, "but I've got a few tricks of my own."

"What do you want me to do?" Jones asked.

"Just watch our prisoners and try to keep a lid on things."

"I'll do that."

"Thanks," Longarm said.

After going to the undertaker's office to pay his last respects to Marshal Walker, Longarm saddled a horse and headed out for Stella's cabin. It would be late before he arrived, but he needed to let the woman know what had transpired this morning and where he was going next. Stella would be upset, but then, so was everyone else in Auburn these dangerous days.

Chapter 14

Stella was waiting when Longarm finally rode his horse up to her cabin. It was almost dark and Longarm was dead tired. Furthermore, he wasn't looking forward to telling Stella that Marshal Jones had been ambushed in the middle of Auburn's main street.

"You look like you've been pulled through a knothole," Stella said, holding a lantern and coming out to help him put away his horse. "What happened?"

"I'll tell you inside," Longarm replied as he forked hay to his played-out mount. "You got any hot food ready? My belly is chewin' on my backbone."

"I have hot coffee, beans, bacon, and I've even managed to make an apple pie," Stella said. "And after that, I'll gladly warm your bed."

He managed a smile. "You're half the reason I'm so wrung out this evening, Stella. But there's something else. Marshal Walker was ambushed and killed right before my eyes."

"Oh, no!" Stella's expression was stricken, and she had to take a deep breath. "Do you know who did it?"

"Yeah," Longarm said. "I shot him dead. Didn't mean to, though. Some of the townspeople, led by an old fella named Fred Potts, stepped forward and identified the killer as a hardcase named Claude Blanton."

"I know him," Stella said. "He's one of Nick's unsavory friends."

"Another man named Art Mead was seen the night before priming Blanton with whiskey, probably to do the killing." Longarm frowned. "Stella, it's looking more and more likely that Nick is behind Noah's death. And who knows, maybe even Abe."

"Nothing would surprise me anymore," she said. "So what are we going to do now?"

"*We* are not going to do anything," Longarm said. "But I mean to go down to Newcastle and see if I can find out more about Claude Blanton. After that, I expect to ride over to Placerville and have a showdown with Art Mead."

"He's a dangerous man, Custis. He carries a hideout derringer up his sleeve and he's—"

"I've heard it all before," Longarm said, placing his fingers over her lips. "But thanks anyway."

"I want to go with you."

"It would be better if you didn't."

"I can't just sit around this cabin for the next few days waiting and wondering what happened!"

"I'm afraid that you'll have to," Longarm told her. "Besides, you're supposed to be languishing in some jail cell down in Sacramento, remember?"

Stella shook her head. "Abe and Nick Huffington know better than that by now. In fact, I wouldn't be surprised if they're rushing back up the mountain this very minute trying to figure out their next move."

"Me neither," Longarm said. "But if I can get Art Mead to confess, then . . ."

"But he *won't* confess!" Stella argued. "Mead is a hard, vicious man, just like Blanton was. Their kind would rather go down shooting than be sent to the prison . . . or risk facing the gallows."

"Well," Longarm replied, "that will be up to Mead. But one way or another we'll have our little talk, and I guarantee you that I'll wring some truth out of him."

"Or die trying," Stella said, looking miserable. "But let's not fret about that now. Come inside and eat, then we'll get you to bed. I can tell that you're not going to be worth all that much to me tonight, but I want you rested when you find Art Mead and demand your answers."

Longarm was glad to sit down and eat his fill. Stella was a very good cook and there was plenty of food to satisfy his appetite. He devoured three quarters of the apple pie, but drank little of the coffee because he needed his sleep.

"Feel better?" she asked when he finally pushed his chair back from his plate.

"Much better."

"Well, then, let's get you undressed and to bed."

Longarm figured he was plenty capable of undressing himself, but Stella had always enjoyed removing his clothes, and tonight, despite the grim circumstances, was no different. When she had him stripped down to his underwear, she threw back the bedcovers.

"Get in while I put a few more sticks of wood in the stove," she ordered.

Longarm climbed into the bed and watched Stella feed the fire, then quickly strip out of her own clothes. She put on a man's cotton nightshirt, but it didn't hide her curves, and when she blew out the lantern and slipped into bed beside him, Longarm quickly realized he wasn't quite as tired as he had imagined.

"Are you sure you're up to this?" Stella asked as he pushed her nightshirt up over her waist and prepared to mount her.

"Yeah," he said, "but this won't be any too strenuous."

"Don't worry," she purred, spreading her legs and receiving his stiff manhood with a sigh of pleasure, "I'll go easy on you tonight."

"Just once," he groaned, feeling her moist heat envelop his pulsing rod. "Just once."

Stella unbuttoned the top of her nightshirt so he could pay attention to her breasts. "We'll see," she murmured as their bodies began to thrust together, "we'll see."

Longarm made love to Stella, then dropped off to sleep and did not awaken until sunrise. Stella was folded tightly against him and he breathed deeply, savoring the smell of her body and the lingering scent of their lovemaking. As the light grew stronger in the cabin, he admired its glow on Stella's hair and wished that he could hold her for an hour or two. But he couldn't. He had to get up, get dressed, and head for Newcastle.

It was chilly outside and there was a patina of frost on the meadow grass when he caught his horse and threw on his saddle. The animal was cantankerous and tried to buck when Longarm swung his leg over the cantle and planted his boots in both stirrups.

"Cut it out, dammit," he growled. "I'm no happier than you are to be leaving at this hour."

The horse set off at a rough trot and, with a last look back, Longarm reined northwest, hoping that the sun would hurry up and lift over the hills to give him some warmth. He rode all morning without a break, and finally intercepted the freighting road that followed the Central Pacific's railroad tracks. He arrived in Newcastle early that afternoon.

Newcastle wasn't much of a town, and Longarm was not sure where to begin his investigation. But then he spotted a ramshackle building whose faded sign said that it was the marshal's office, and decided that it would be best to report in and state his business. Quite often, the local authorities were more trouble than help, and it wasn't unusual to find them resentful of federal officers, but Longarm hoped that would not be the case today.

When he stepped into the office, a sloppy-looking man with a three-day-old beard and food stains dotting his shirt glanced up from his newspaper.

"Are you the marshal?" Longarm finally asked.

"Might be. What'cha want?"

"I'm United States Deputy Marshal Custis Long. I'm working on a case and need some information on a fella named Claude Blanton. Can you help me?"

"My name is Amos Hackett. Marshal Amos T. Hackett," the unkempt man said, struggling out of his broken chair and looking Longarm over. "So, you're a *Fed,* huh?"

"That's right."

"What kind of a 'case' would you be working on and what do you want to know about Blanton?"

Longarm could see the suspicion in Hackett's eyes. All too often when a federal officer arrived, either the local authorities were envious, or else they started looking for a reward or some personal gain. And this man looked hungrier than most.

"He ambushed Marshal Walker in Auburn," Longarm

said. "I had to kill him before I could find out why."

"Claude shot old Pete Walker?"

Longarm saw no sign that Hackett was either surprised or particularly upset by this news. "That's right. Walker's dead. I'm trying to find out why Blanton would do such a thing."

"Claude was mean and he'd probably been drinking," Hackett answered. "He hated most everyone. I sure never trusted to turn my back on him."

Longarm frowned. "He was seen drinking with another hardcase named Art Mead. I'm told that they were friends."

"Not friends," Hackett corrected. "They were just a couple of sonsabitches that worked together when there was money to be made. Claude Blanton was no damned good, but since he's dead, what do you want here now?"

"Maybe someone he knows could help me pin a conspiracy on Art Mead and anyone else that might have had a hand in Marshal Walker's assassination," Longarm replied. "I don't know. I just have a feeling that the ambush was more than a simple vendetta between Blanton and Walker. In fact, it's been reported to me that Mead was buying Blanton all the whiskey he could handle the night before the ambush."

"I know Mead. I wished you'd have gunned him down along with Blanton."

"What about Nick Huffington?" Longarm asked. "Could be there was some connection."

"I doubt that," the marshal said. "After all, why would anyone with the name of Huffington have anything to do with murdering a marshal?"

"Money," Longarm said simply. "And it all ties back to the murder of Noah Huffington. Abe Huffington's favored son."

"I heard that he was stabbed to death by that woman he took up with. Her names was . . ."

"Her name is Miss Stella Vacarro," Longarm said, "and I guarantee you she had nothing to do with Noah's death."

"I don't see how you can be so sure of that," the marshal said pointedly. "After all, she'd stabbed a man to death before with a stiletto."

Longarm shook his head. "Did Claude Blanton have any family that I should notify?"

"He lived with a woman and some kids just south of town. Their place is real hard to find and you've never seen a sorrier family."

"Well," Longarm decided, "sorry or not, I ought to inform them that Claude is dead."

"You might get your ass shot off for your trouble," Hackett warned. "The woman is a witch and her boys are going to grow up to be troublemakers . . . or worse."

"Why don't you put on your hat and take me out there?" Longarm suggested.

Hackett shook his head. "Well, I really ought to stay here in town in case there's trouble."

"That doesn't seem too likely," Longarm replied with growing annoyance. "It's a real small town and I doubt this little errand would take more than an hour—if we get started right away."

Hackett didn't want to be bothered. "I . . ."

"There might be a reward," Longarm said, dangling his lure. "Sometimes there is when a lawman is murdered."

"For what? You already killed Claude."

Longarm could see that the man wasn't going to take the bait. He was a discredit to the profession, but not entirely stupid. "All right, I'll pay you five dollars to take me out to this woman's house."

"House?" Hackett scoffed. "Even calling it a shack is an exaggeration. It's just a collection of rusty tin and broken wood that they stole from the railroad sheds. It's all held together with chicken wire."

"Five dollars," Longarm repeated, pulling a bill out of his pocket and holding it up before the marshal.

"All right," Hackett said, reaching for the money.

Longarm pulled it away saying, "You'll get paid when we leave the woman."

"You ain't a bit trusting, are you?" Hackett snapped.

"No," Longarm replied, "I'm not. Let's get moving."

"Why don't you pay me three dollars and I'll tell that witch the next time she comes into town?" Hackett suggested. "That way, you save yourself two dollars and we don't go to the bother of riding out there and having to put up with that bunch of trash."

"No," Longarm insisted. "The woman lived with Blanton. She at least has the right to hear that he's never coming back."

"She'd hear it even if we didn't tell her."

"Get your hat and move!" Longarm said, putting steel into his voice.

"All right, all right!"

It took Hackett nearly an hour to get someone to give him the use of a horse. He was so fat that the horse had to be especially stout, and he had a devil of a time getting into the saddle. But at last they rode out of Newcastle and followed the road south for about three miles. Once, the train passed them and a lot of passengers waved from the windows. Longarm was in a sour mood and ignored them, but Hackett had to stop his horse and wave until the train and its passengers were all out of sight.

"I try to be friendly to folks," Hackett explained as they continued on down the road. "It helps, you know."

"It also helps to keep yourself fit and clean," Longarm said.

Hackett bristled. "Just because I work for a little town and they don't hardly pay me enough to live on is no reason to be insulting."

"How much further?"

"About two miles. We leave this road and take a trail off to the south. You can start to smell these people about then."

Longarm didn't say anything. Hackett didn't say anything more either, and so they rode in irritable silence all the way to the shack where Claude Blanton's woman and her kids lived.

"There it is," Hackett said, pointing through the trees. "They got some big, mean hounds, so don't dismount or they're likely to chew your leg off."

Longarm pushed on ahead. Suddenly, a pack of hounds began to howl as they came flying out from under a broken-down wagon. There were six or seven of them, all big and mangy. About the same number of children, ranging from toddlers to kids in their teens, came chasing after the hounds.

"Ain't it a chillin' sight," Hackett said with disgust. "They're all ornery little beggars. Just stay on your horse and don't worry about quirting them in the face if they get too close."

Since Hackett held back, Longarm rode forward, and the dogs swirled in around his horse causing it to have fits. Then the kids arrived and it was a melee, but Longarm kept riding until he drew to within fifty feet of the run-down shack.

Hackett hadn't been exaggerating when he said it was a sorry sight. There was garbage all over the yard and the shack itself wasn't fit for human habitation.

"Hello the house!" Longarm shouted.

A woman as wide as the door itself appeared with a shotgun clenched in her fists. She was so obese and filthy that she made Marshal Hackett appear fastidious.

"What the hell you want!" she screamed through a mouth mostly without teeth.

"Ma'am," Longarm said, "I have something important to tell you, but I won't say it while you're holding that shotgun on me and Marshal Hackett."

"You a lawman too?"

"I'm Marshal Long."

"I *hate* lawmen!"

Longarm's hand eased closer to his pistol and, out of the corner of his eye, he could see that Hackett was sweating profusely.

"What I have to tell you is important, ma'am. Put the shotgun down."

The woman spat at her bare and dirty feet. She lowered the shotgun and yelled, "Speak your piece and then get outa my sight, you murderin' maggots!"

Longarm was having second thoughts about this mission, and realized why Hackett had been so reluctant to come out here despite the enticement of money. But second-guessing wasn't going to help, so he just drew his six-gun and shouted, "Claude is dead. He ambushed Marshal Walker in Auburn and I had no choice but to kill him or he would have killed me too."

The woman's jaw dropped. Her chins quivered, and Longarm was sure she was going to try and kill him, but instead, she threw back her head and howled with joy, then began to cackle.

"I told you that she was a damned witch," Hackett said, mopping his greasy face with a dirty handkerchief. "Crazier than a loon."

Longarm was willing to agree, but mostly he was just glad that he wasn't going to have to use his pistol.

"Ma'am? Ma'am," he said when the laughter finally started to die. "I'd like to know what's so funny."

The woman had started to cough, and when she could catch her breath, she looked up and said, "What's funny is that I'd made up my mind to kill Claude *myself*! The son-ofabitch was *cheatin'* on me!"

"Let's get out of here," Hackett muttered. "Maybe whatever ails her is contagious."

But Longarm shook his head. "Ma'am, did he ever tell you that he was going to try and kill Marshal Walker?"

The woman was red in the face, but she managed to nod her head and say, "Not exactly. Not the marshal anyway."

"What do you mean?"

"He was supposed to kill Noah Huffington with a stiletto. Did he do it?"

Longarm took a deep breath. "Are you saying that he was talking about murdering Noah Huffington?"

"Yeah. With Art Mead and Nick Huffington. I got some of Claude's money after they all got drunk! Stole it right out of Claude's pockets! He promised to give me more, but he spent it on some whore. That's why I was going to kill the cheatin' sonofabitch!"

Longarm knew that he finally had the evidence he needed to arrest Mead and Nick Huffington—if this harridan would testify in court and if she could be believed by a judge or jury, which was doubtful.

"Ma'am," Longarm said, digging into his pockets but not trusting the hounds enough to dismount. "Here is twenty dollars. Buy yourself a dress and some shoes."

The woman just stared at him. "Why?"

"You're going to testify to what you heard in a court of law."

"Not for no twenty dollars, I'm not!"

"All right," Longarm said, "then it could be a lot more."

"*You* payin' me?"

"No, but I promise that you and your kids will be generously *helped,* if you just tell the truth and repeat the conversation that you overheard between Claude, Mead, and Huffington."

"You want me to say *they* plotted to murder that rich Auburn preacher?"

"That's right."

The woman gazed out at her kids, her dirty face reflecting powerful emotions. "We got it real hard here, Mr. Lawman. I reckon you can see how hard my kids got it. Everyone else in these parts looks down their damn snotty noses at my family."

"You can leave this behind and start over," Longarm said, knowing he would have to worry about the money later. Stella would no doubt help. She had the money and the heart of gold. She'd help, all right.

"Maybe a *real* house for us," the woman said quietly. "Nothing fancy, mind you. Just a *real* house with a roof that didn't leak and walls that kept out the winter wind."

"You deserve that much," Longarm assured her.

"Maybe I don't, but my kids do. Claude wasn't good to

'em. The youngest are his, but he treated them like dirt. I hated Claude. He wasn't much of a man anymore, not around here and not even in bed.''

"You could go away and start over fresh," Longarm said. "There's nothing here worth staying for."

Hackett hissed, "Let's get the hell out of here!"

"I'll be back," Longarm promised the woman.

"When?"

"I don't know."

"Maybe you'll just kill Art and Nick like you did Claude. If you kill 'em, you wouldn't need me, would you."

"Here's twenty dollars," Longarm said, handing the money to one of the grubby children. "There will be more."

And then, with Hackett close on his heels, Longarm rode away.

Chapter 15

"Hey!" Marshal Hackett shouted, flogging his horse in an attempt to overtake Longarm. "Wait up, dammit!"

Longarm reined in for a moment to let Hackett catch him. He had a strong dislike for the man because he was only interested in a personal reward rather than in seeking justice.

"What is it now?" Longarm asked impatiently.

"You offered that witch money!"

"That's right."

"Where's my five dollars for bringing you out here?"

"Sorry, that twenty was all that I had."

"Dammit, why'd you give her my money?"

"Because I never saw a family that needed it more and I have a friend who has been falsely accused of murdering Noah Huffington. I'm sure that she'll be more than happy to show her appreciation for any testimony that woman can provide."

"I'll testify to what I heard her say! You can count on me, Marshal Long."

"I'll keep that in mind."

"We got 'em!" Hackett said excitedly. "Ain't no doubt about that now!"

"Yes, there is," Longarm countered. "That woman could be lying."

"Hell, she's telling the truth! Why, even a blind man could see that."

"Don't be so sure," Longarm said. "It's very clear that she hated Claude Blanton and his friends. Hated them enough to say most anything out of spite."

"I suppose. But we could probably twist a few of them dirty little arms and also get them older kids to back up whatever their mother says."

Longarm gave the man a look of disgust. "You've no scruples at all, have you."

"No what?"

"Never mind," Longarm snapped. "But we're not going to force testimony out of anyone—big or small."

"Just an idea," Hackett grumbled. "No reason to get all huffy about it. So what are we going to do now? Ride over to Placerville and arrest Art Mead?"

"That's the general idea," Longarm replied. "Given his bad reputation, the man shouldn't be very hard to find."

"I'll be ready to back you up."

"I think," Longarm said slowly, "that you don't need to bother. I work best alone."

"Oh, no! If it hadn't been for me, you wouldn't ever have found that witch, let alone got her to tie Nick Huffington and Art Mead into the murder."

"I'd have found her, with or without you," Longarm said. "When we get back to Newcastle, return to your office and stay there where you belong."

Hackett's jaw sagged. "And let you take all the credit and reward! Ha! I'm . . ."

Longarm had more than enough of this reprehensible character. He reached out and backhanded Hackett across the side of his fat face so hard that he rocked the pathetic lawman back in his saddle.

"Owww!" Hackett bawled, dropping his reins and cradling his head in his hands. "What'd you do *that* for!"

"I did it because I resent you thinking that we're both out here for the same selfish reasons. We're not! You want a cash reward. I want justice and to clear the name of my friend."

"You mean that fancy whore named . . ."

Before Longarm could belt Hackett again, the man spurred off toward Newcastle.

"Good riddance," Longarm grumbled, anxious to find the first road that would take him to Placerville and Art Mead.

Placerville was located about twenty miles southeast of Auburn. According to a sign posted just outside town, in 1848 Placerville had been the site of a big gold discovery by three prospectors who quickly excavated almost twenty thousand dollars. The following year, thousands of miners had staked out every gulch and hillside and dubbed the settlement "Dry Diggings," but then they changed that name after a series of highly popular lynchings to "Hangtown."

Longarm read that more than fifty million dollars worth of gold had already been mined from the surrounding hills, and that the famous Central Pacific Railroad tycoons Mark Hopkins and Collis P. Huntington had both gotten their start as Placerville merchants.

"Hey there!" Longarm called to a passing horseman. "Can you give me some information?"

The man reined in his mount. He was young, and Longarm noticed that he warily kept his right hand close to his gun. "What kind of information, stranger?"

"I'm looking for Art Mead. Do you know where I can find him?"

"Probably in the Big Pine Saloon." The young man studied Longarm with suspicion. "Are you a friend?"

"Nope."

"Well," the rider said, "if you're an enemy, I wish you all the luck because you'll need it in order to stay alive. Mead is dangerous, especially when he's had a few drinks—which is most of the time."

"If he's as dangerous and troublesome as everyone tells me, then why doesn't the town marshal step in and do something about him?"

"Because Art Mead has already gunned him down."

"Oh. Well, that explains it then. And thanks for the warning."

"You take my advice, you forget about whatever trouble you have with Art Mead. Write it off to experience. That's better than getting killed."

"Thanks for the advice," Longarm said, nodding his appreciation for the man's time before he continued on down the road and into Placerville.

The town was impressive. The sign had also said that the early settlements of Dry Diggings and Hangtown had repeatedly been razed by fire, and so now all of Placerville's buildings were constructed of rock and brick. The settlement's most notable structures were its fine City Hall, the Zeisz Brewery, a handsome Victorian mansion offering rooms on Cedar Street, and the Episcopal church, built in the shape of an inverted ship's hull.

Many of the downtown businesses, however, were closed and boarded up, telling Longarm that Placerville was now in a period of slow economic decline. No doubt its rich deposits of ore were playing out, despite the evidence of hydraulic mining which had left the nearby western Sierra slopes as bare and bleeding as open ulcers.

The Big Pine Saloon was situated almost in the center of town, and so Longarm tied his horse to the nearest empty hitching rail and checked his six-gun. At times like this, he never gave his quarry advance warning by wearing his badge. Instead, he kept it out of sight until it was really needed. Longarm reminded himself that Mead had that derringer hidden up his sleeve and that the man had a reputation for being very quick and very deadly.

Well, he thought, I will take no unnecessary chances, but I do want a confession from this man and for that I need him alive.

The Big Pine Saloon looked like a thousand other watering holes in the West. It had bars across the front windows and bat-wing doors that were about to drop off their hinges. The building was poorly constructed with dirty, tobacco-stained sawdust spread across a floor that reeked of urine and vomit. The place was dim and the smoke was thick.

Longarm stood just inside the door for a few moments until his eyes adjusted. Then he began to survey the room, chiding himself for not having a much better physical description of Art Mead. All he knew was that the man had a big scar on his face and was a gunfighter, which therefore meant he would be wearing a fast-draw rig.

Three men at the bar, their backs turned to Longarm, fit

Art Mead's general description, but two of them were drinking together. Longarm decided that the loner was probably his man. Unbuttoning his coat, he pushed it back a little so that the butt of his gun was in easy reach. Longarm's side arm was a double-action .44-.40 Colt revolver which he wore on his left hip. Most men preferred to draw from their right side, but Longarm liked the cross-draw and it had served him well enough in the past so that he was not about to change.

As Longarm started across the room toward the loner, he noted that the Big Pine Saloon was packed, which was both good and bad. Good because the crowd obscured his arrival, but bad because there were just too many hard drinkers that might want to get involved in a gunfight. Normally, if bullets started to fly, intelligent and sober men would be smart enough to hit the floor or dive for cover. But in a tough saloon like the Big Pine, you could toss out that theory because there were always a few drunken fools willing to become dead heroes.

Longarm slipped in next to his suspect, but did not look directly at the man. "I'll have a nickel beer," he called to a hustling bartender.

"Be right with you!"

Then Longarm looked closer at his most likely suspect, and noted the terrible knife scar across his face. This was Art Mead, all right.

"How's the beer here?" he asked Mead, trying to sound relaxed and cordial.

"What?"

"The beer? Is it good . . . or green?"

Mead shook his head, and Longarm could hear the meanness in his voice when he growled, "Stranger, if you ain't

162

man enough to drink what's served, then you'd best get your picky ass outa here."

"I was just askin'," Longarm said in his most apologetic tone as he extracted a nickel from his pocket and placed it on the bar in front of him. He looked at Mead again and said, "Haven't we met before?"

"No and we ain't met now," Mead hissed. "So shut up and leave me the hell alone."

"I was just trying to make some social conversation," Longarm said. "What's the matter, having a bad day or something?"

The man on the other side of Longarm elbowed him sharply in the ribs. "You better just shut your mouth, mister. Art ain't one to pester."

"I'm not pestering him," Longarm said. "I was just trying to be friendly."

"Well, *don't*," the man said, looking nervous. "Otherwise, someone might get shot by accident and it might even be *me*."

"Oh."

The bartender brought Longarm his beer and took the nickel. Longarm picked up his mug and tasted his warm beer. He smacked his lips and made a sour face, saying, "It's green as grass, dammit!"

Mead had a very short fuse and his patience was about to run out, which was just what Longarm intended. Playing the harmless fool, Longarm was attempting to prod Mead into stepping outside with him to fight. That way, he could hope to catch the man off guard and alone so he could be arrested and no one in the crowded saloon would be shot by accident.

"I said that the beer was *green*," Longarm repeated to

Mead. "If you'd have been helpful enough to warn me of the fact, I'd have tried whiskey instead."

"You big, stupid bastard!" Mead growled low in his throat. "I've had all the lip from you I can stand!"

Longarm pretended to be surprised, hurt, and even a little offended. "Well, I was only . . ."

Mead didn't let Longarm finish, but grabbed him by the arm and propelled him toward the bat-wing doors. It was easy enough to let himself be hustled through the crowd, and Longarm suspected that, once outside, Mead would try to beat him to a pulp in order to remind everyone of his toughness.

"Look," Longarm protested as they both plowed across the saloon. "I don't know what all this trouble is about. I really didn't mean to upset you."

"I'm going to teach you a lesson you should have learned a long, long time ago," Mead swore as he balled his fists and shoved Longarm outside. "I'm going to feed you your gawddamn teeth!"

Longarm raised his hands as if to protect himself and then, when Mead threw a haymaker at his face, he ducked the powerful punch and drove an uppercut to Mead's belly that raised him a good foot off the ground.

Mead's eyes bugged with pain. He choked and his hand flashed for the fancy ivory-handled Colt at his side. Longarm batted it from his grasp, then unleashed a wicked right cross that snapped Mead's head around and sent him backpedaling. Rather than give the gunfighter any opportunity to recover, Longarm waded in with both fists and punished Art Mead with one thundering blow after another. He pulped Mead's nose like a stomped grape, then broke his lips and opened a huge gash over his left eye causing Mead to bleed heavily.

164

Longarm hit Mead until he slammed up against a storefront wall and tried to pull out the hideout derringer from under his sleeve.

Longarm jumped in and grabbed Mead's right arm with both hands, then slammed it down across his rising knee. Mead howled. Yanking the gunfighter's other sleeve up, Longarm disarmed him, then kicked his legs out from under him so that Mead toppled to the dirt.

He grabbed Mead by the shirtfront, dragged him erect, and shook him like a rag doll while yelling into his bloody face, "My name is *Federal Deputy Marshal* Custis Long and I'm putting you under arrest."

"What for!"

"For the murder of Noah Huffington and Marshal Pete Walker of Auburn."

"I didn't kill them! I got witnesses that'll say I was right here in Placerville when they both got theirs!"

"Sure," Longarm growled, "but you got Claude Blanton drunk and talked him into doing your murdering, didn't you!"

"You're crazy!" Mead screeched. "Gawdammit, you near broke my arm! You can't do this to innocent folks!"

"You're about as innocent as Billy the Kid." Longarm searched the man for any more weapons. He found a knife and tossed it away saying, "Where's your horse?"

"What the hell do you want my horse for!"

"I'm taking you to Auburn, where you'll be tried and almost sure to be found guilty. You might not get the gallows, but you'll sure as hell grow old in prison for being an accomplice to murder."

"Oh, yeah? I got friends that will get me a lawyer! You

165

ain't got nothing on me, Marshal. We'll have your gawdamn badge for this!''

"We'll see," Longarm said through clenched teeth. "We'll just see."

Chapter 16

When Longarm returned to Auburn with his prisoner, the townspeople turned out to give him a hearty welcome. They knew Mead, and they were all grinning when they saw that he was handcuffed and headed for jail.

"Congratulations, Marshal Long!" a man said, coming up to slap Longarm on the back. "It sure is good to see that Mead is finally going to get his long-overdue reward in Hell."

"Well," Longarm said, dragging his prisoner from his horse and shoving him toward the marshal's office, "whatever happens to him is up to a judge and a jury."

Marshal Jones had the door open wide, and he wasted no time in putting Mead in a cell.

"What happened to the other two prisoners?" Longarm asked.

"They were sentenced and hanged yesterday," Jones answered. "You missed quite a show, but I expect that this one will make up for it when he dances in the wind."

Mead, his face purple and swollen from the effects of the beating he'd taken from Longarm, shivered but managed to keep up his bravado by hissing, "The Huffingtons ain't going to let me swing. They'll get me off."

"I don't think so," Longarm replied, collapsing in Pete Walker's old office chair and then kicking his boots up on the desk. "We've got a witness that will testify that you, Claude Blanton, and Nick Huffington were all in cahoots. That you plotted to murder Noah Huffington and then ambush Marshal Walker. You'll swing, all right."

"What witness?"

"You'll find out soon enough."

Mead turned around and went over to sit on the cell bunk. He cradled his head in his hands for a moment, then looked up to say, "I need a good lawyer. I want to see Mr. Abe Huffington!"

"If he comes by," Marshal Jones said, "we'll pass along the message. But we don't have time to go hunt up the man."

"I want a *lawyer*!"

"You'll have one," Longarm promised. "But it won't change the fact that you're going to hang."

Mead's head almost dropped between his knees, and he muttered something to himself that Longarm could not decipher.

"What'd you say?"

Mead's head snapped up. "What if . . . ah, never mind."

"What if what?" Longarm said, dropping his boots to the floor and going over to stand beside the cell. "Are you thinking about cutting a deal in exchange for your life?"

Mead didn't look up, but when he spoke, his voice broke. "Maybe."

Longarm glanced over his shoulder at Marshal Jones, who just shrugged as if he didn't care much one way or the other. Longarm turned his attention back to the prisoner.

"Was Abe Huffington involved in the murder of his son Noah or Marshal Walker?"

"No!" Mead looked up. "But you tell Abe he better come and take care of me!"

"Why?" Longarm said. "He's a very busy and important man. What if he isn't interested in your problems?"

"He'd *better* be!"

"Why?" Longarm repeated.

" 'Cause I ain't going to no gallows while Nick Huffington goes scot free!"

"So you admit that he was in on the murders."

"I didn't say that."

"Not exactly," Longarm admitted, "but close enough. Where is Nick right now?"

"I don't know."

"I think that you probably do."

Mead shook his head and began to pace back and forth in his cell. Then, he stopped and spun around to point at Longarm. "I *know* who's been talking! It's Agnes!"

"Who is she?"

"Agnes was Claude Blanton's woman. She lives in that shack outside of Newcastle and she's got all them damn kids and dogs. *She's* the one that opened her big mouth, isn't she!"

"No," Longarm lied.

"The hell you say! It *has* to be Agnes!"

The very last thing that Longarm wanted was for this man to somehow get the word out to Nick Huffington that Agnes had betrayed them. If he did that, then the woman's life would be in grave danger.

"How about a signed confession right now?" Longarm offered. "In exchange for my recommendation that you be given life in prison instead of the death sentence.''

''Not a chance!'' Mead became very agitated. ''I want to see Mr. Huffington and I want a good lawyer! I ain't saying nothing more.''

To emphasize his words, Mead stomped over to flop down on his bunk. He pulled his hat low over his eyes and pretended to go to sleep saying, ''Wake me when I have visitors.''

Longarm turned from the cell and motioned for Marshal Jones to follow him outside.

''Trouble?'' Jones asked when they were alone and could talk privately.

''I'm afraid so. Mead is no fool. He was right in guessing that Agnes, the Newcastle woman, is the one who told me about the murder plot.''

''I see.'' Jones frowned. ''But what can Mead do to silence her if he's in jail?''

''Nothing,'' Longarm said. ''But if he somehow gets word to Nick Huffington, Agnes is as good as dead. And even worse, Nick might decide to kill her children too so there wouldn't be any witnesses.''

''Holy shit!'' Jones exclaimed. ''I see what you mean. What are we going to do if Abe Huffington comes here? Or a lawyer? We can't legally keep Mead isolated.''

''I know,'' Longarm said, thinking hard. ''And I have a feeling that Huffington will show up pretty soon. When he does, we'll just let him visit with Mead. It ought to be an interesting conversation and tell me a great deal about whether or not Abe has been involved in these murders.''

''But what if Mead tells him about Agnes?''

''Then Huffington will have to make a decision. He'll either allow his only surviving son to go to the gallows exactly as he deserves—or he'll pass the word along to Nick to head for Newcastle to kill Agnes.''

"And if Abe makes that choice, you'll be able to arrest him.''

"Exactly!'' Longarm went back inside and over to stretch out on Pete Walker's bunk saying, "Like Mead, I'm going to take a nap. Wake me when we have visitors.''

"*Any* visitors?''

"Yeah,'' Longarm said, closing his eyes. "Anyone at all.''

Longarm didn't need to be awakened when Abe Huffington stormed in a few hours later. The politician was furious, disheveled, and badly shaken. He was also accompanied by a nattily dressed Sacramento lawyer.

"My client, Mr. Abraham Huffington, demands to talk to your prisoner in strict confidence,'' the lawyer announced.

Jones glanced over at Longarm, who sat up sleepily and rubbed his eyes with his knuckles. He yawned, scratched, and said, "All right. Marshal Jones, open the cell and let these men have their little powwow with the condemned man.''

"I *resent* that remark!'' the lawyer snapped.

"Well, that's quite a coincidence,'' Longarm said, "because I'm already starting to resent *you.*''

"You're finished as a federal officer,'' Huffington passionately vowed. "You've run roughshod over everyone in Auburn and I'm going to do everything in my power to see that . . .''

"Oh,'' Longarm said, coming to his feet. "You mean, *if* you are elected the governor of California, you will try to get me fired.''

"That's exactly right."

"Well, Mr. Huffington, let me fill you in on a thing or two. In the first place, your political career is definitely finished. And in the second place, if you had *anything* to do with these murders, the only career you can look forward to is a life in prison!"

Huffington was well past his physical prime, but he almost attacked Longarm anyway, so great was his fury. But his attorney managed to hold him off and then get him pointed toward the cell.

"We'd like *strict* privacy here," the lawyer said, emphasizing the word.

"Well," Longarm replied, "we're not leaving this office, if that's what you have in mind. So I guess that you'll just have to put your damned heads together and whisper like a bunch of schoolchildren."

"That man is finished!" Huffington raged. "Finished!"

Longarm grinned. If he could prod Abe Huffington into attacking him, then he would be able to deck the offensive sonofabitch as well as put him under arrest for assaulting an officer of the law. That would suit Longarm right down to the ground.

The lawyer understood this, and was able to calm Huffington until they were both ushered inside Mead's cell. Longarm took the precaution of locking the cell behind them, and then he went back to sit and wait. Without any preamble, Mead, Huffington, and the lawyer put their heads together and began to confer in frantic whispers.

Longarm jammed an unlit cheroot into his mouth and offered one to Marshal Jones, who declined it. They both watched the huddled group of men with a mixture of amusement and interest. Longarm couldn't overhear what was being discussed, but he had a pretty good idea. What he did not yet know was if Abe Huffington had any prior knowledge of the murder of his son or of the ambush of Pete Walker.

"You murdering fool!" Huffington suddenly exploded.

Before anyone could react, the older man attacked the already badly beaten Art Mead. The powerful Huffington sledged his huge fists into Mead's purple and swollen face, then grabbed the dazed prisoner by the hair and smashed his skull over and over against the cell's rock wall in a series of sickening thuds.

Bright red blood trickled from Art Mead's ears and mouth. His body went limp, but Huffington was crazy and kept pounding his head into the stone.

"Marshal!" the lawyer shrieked as he tried vainly to pull Abe Huffington away. "Help!"

It took Longarm a few seconds to get the cell door unlocked. When he did, it required all of his strength to drag Abe Huffington off the unconscious prisoner, then knock him practically senseless, before the big politician was finally subdued.

Ashen-faced, the lawyer bolted out of the cell and began to vomit on the floor. Marshal Jones rushed past Longarm to Art Mead's side. He felt for a pulse, but it was missing. He placed his ear to Mead's chest, listened carefully, then shook his head.

"Mead is dead."

"Well," Longarm said, studying Abe Huffington, "then we've got a new prisoner to charge with murder. Abe, get up!"

Huffington was still on his knees, head bent, now sobbing.

Longarm motioned Jones to help him drag Art Mead's body out of the cell. When that was done, Longarm went back into the cell and stood over Abe Huffington.

"So," he said, "you *weren't* an accomplice to the murders."

"Hell, no!" Huffington choked. "I loved Noah!"

"But he was going to marry Miss Vacarro and that could have derailed your political career. Maybe you just couldn't bear that possibility."

Huffington looked up, and his beefy face was a mask of twisted grief. "I'd *never* kill my own son!"

"But you just killed Art Mead. And Nick was a part of the plot to murder Noah. Mr. Huffington, you can say goodbye to becoming California's next governor. Even with a sharp attorney, you're going to go to prison for a long time and your murdering son Nick is going to the gallows."

Huffington sobbed again, then pulled a handkerchief out of his coat pocket and blew his nose. "I want Nick to burn in Hell for his role in killing Noah!"

The lawyer shouted, "Don't say another word, Mr. Huffington! Not a single word!"

"Why?" Huffington cried. "That scum told us everything. I knew Nick was wild and had a mean streak, but I *never* believed that he would be a part of murdering his own brother! Blanton actually stabbed Noah to death, but they—"

"Mr. Huffington, I *beg* you!" the lawyer wailed. "Say nothing more!"

"You'd probably better listen to your attorney," Longarm advised. "But for what it's worth, there's no doubt in my mind that you didn't have anything to do with murdering Marshal Walker—or your son. Instead, you just killed our prisoner, and you're now under arrest for murder."

Longarm stepped outside the cell and looked at the attorney. "You want back in there to advise your client?"

"No," the attorney said in a trembling voice as he gazed vacantly down at his white shirt, now stained with fresh blood and flecks of his own vomit. "There doesn't seem to be a lot of point in that at the moment, does there."

"I don't think so," Longarm replied. "Do you know where I can find and arrest Nick?"

"No."

"I do." Huffington raised his head. He appeared to have aged ten years in the last ten minutes.

"Mr. Huffington, please don't say anything more!" the attorney begged.

"Nick is on his way to Newcastle."

Longarm's blood went cold. "To murder Agnes."

"I don't know why he's going there," Huffington said. "I just know that's where he's gone."

Longarm shot a glance at Marshal Jones. "How could Mead have gotten word to Nick about our Newcastle witness!"

"I don't know," Jones replied, throwing up his hands. "While you were taking a nap, there were no visitors, but Mead did wake up and ask for a paper and pencil. Said he wanted to write down the name of an attorney . . . or some such thing."

"An attorney?" Longarm shook his head. "I'll bet anything he wrote a note to Nick and tossed it through the bars of his cell window. And the note would have told Nick about Agnes being the key to a conviction. *That's* why Nick is on his way to Newcastle!"

Longarm sprinted for the door. He *had* to get to Newcastle in a hurry, or that poor, wretched woman and her children were as good as dead.

Chapter 17

Longarm barreled out the door and grabbed his horse. He swung into the saddle and rode hard for Newcastle. It was only three miles down the line, but he realized that he would have to ride another couple of miles more in order to reach Agnes's shack.

Longarm blamed himself for taking a short nap. Had he stayed awake, he would have seen through Art Mead's request for writing materials. Tragically, his mistake just might have cost Agnes and perhaps even her brood of children their lives.

It seemed to take forever to reach Newcastle, and a lot of heads turned as Longarm galloped hard on through town heading west toward the turnoff that would bring him to Agnes's dilapidated shack.

Longarm could hear the pack of hounds as soon as he turned off the main road and started down the narrow, winding lane toward the woman's shack. The dogs sounded so mournful that the hair stood up on the back of Longarm's neck. He forced his exhausted mount down the lane, and when he burst into the clearing, he saw Nick Huffington standing in the middle of the yard. Agnes was sprawled across her porch, lifeless hands clutching her shotgun. Longarm saw dead hounds scattered all over the yard, two of them howling in agony, gutshot and slowly dying.

He saw no children's bodies, and realized that they had probably scattered like frightened quail into the forest. Nick was preparing to go hunt them down and kill them too.

"You're under arrest!" Longarm shouted, drawing his six-gun.

Nick unleashed a bullet that struck Longarm's horse squarely in the chest. The running animal did a somersault that catapulted Longarm over its head. He hit the ground and tried to roll, but struck a rock. His Colt was knocked flying into the brush.

Nick fired again, and Longarm felt hot lead scorch the side of his head. He almost lost consciousness, and tried to scramble to his feet, but was too dazed. Longarm figured he was probably going to die in the next second or two. Lying on his stomach, he wormed his hand in under his coat and palmed the derringer that was attached to his watch fob and chain. It was a solid brass, twin-barrel .44 and it had saved Longarm's bacon more than once. He prayed that it would save him again.

"You sonofabitch!" Nick swore as he advanced. "Gawdamn am I glad to see *you*."

Longarm raised his head to see Nick standing over him with his gun cocked and ready to blow his brains out. There was no time to think so Longarm just blurted out the first thing that came to mind. "Nick, your father knows you had a hand in killing your brother."

"No!" Nick actually staggered backward.

"Yeah," Longarm gritted out, raising his chest a little so

that he could move the derringer into a better firing position. "And I've got some more bad news."

Nick extended the gun down toward Longarm's head, his eyes burning with hatred, his lips twisted in a cold, triumphant sneer. "What are you going to say before I put a bullet in your head, Marshal?"

Icy fear prickled Longarm's skin, but he kept his voice steady. "When your father found everything out, he killed Art Mead. He's going to go to prison for murder."

Nick blinked. "My father *killed* Art? How!"

"He beat his brains out against the jail cell wall. Mead had already told us that you were part of the murder plot."

"You're lying!"

"Every lawman in northern California will be looking for you," Longarm said. "And your father's money will be tied up forever in court. You're coming out of this with nothing but a ticket to a hangman's party."

"I don't believe you!" Nick raged, the Colt beginning to shake in his fist.

Longarm knew that he had run out of time, and he didn't see how on earth he was going to save his life. Still, he could try, and . . .

The blast of a double-barreled shotgun cut across the clearing like the roar of a Kansas tornado. Longarm saw Nick Huffington take both loads of shot between his shoulder blades and slam forward, dead before he struck the ground. Longarm glanced toward the shack to see a barefoot boy who could not have been more than twelve holding his mother's smoking shotgun. The boy dropped the smoking weapon and sprinted around the shack and into the woods.

Longarm released his derringer and tried to gather his wits. After a few minutes, he pushed himself to his feet. He swayed dizzily over to the shack and collected the still-smoking shotgun. Then, he sat down on the broken porch and rested his head in his hands.

Let me see, he thought. Agnes is dead and so is Nick, Claude Blanton, and Art Mead. The two train robbers were hanged yesterday. I guess that wraps it up. But now what?

"Mister?"

Longarm raised his head, feeling the warm blood trickling down his cheek. A little girl with dusty, tearstained cheeks was holding a filthy handkerchief out to him.

"Mister," she said, "you're awful hurt."

Longarm took the handkerchief and pressed it to his throbbing scalp wound. "Yeah," he said, "I guess I am, but I'll feel better soon."

"He killed Mommy!" the child wailed, and burst into fresh tears.

Longarm gently placed a hand on the little girl's shoulder. She threw herself into his arms and cried as if there were no tomorrow. "Your mother was brave," Longarm told her. "And God took her to heaven."

"Is he taking *us* to heaven too?"

"Not yet. Not for a long, long time."

"Then where are we going to go?"

Longarm stared out at the dead dogs, the dead horse, and that dead sonofabitch Nick. This was no place for kids. Never had been and never would be.

"Have you ever heard of a place called Denver?"

"No."

"It's in a state called Colorado. You ever hear of that?"

"No. Is it like heaven?" She sniffled and brightened a little.

"Well, sorta. That's where we're all going now."

"But I don't have no mommy no more!"

Longarm thought of Stella Vacarro. Stella with the heart of gold and a deep, abiding need to give and receive so much love. "I've got someone that will take real good care of you in Denver," he promised, "someone as good and pretty as an angel."

His words pleased and reassured the little girl. So much so that she hugged his neck tightly while Longarm watched her brothers and sisters slowly emerge into the yard like frightened forest elves.

"It's all going to be all right now," Longarm vowed in a voice that betrayed his powerful emotions. "And that's a promise."

Watch for

**LONGARM AND THE RENEGADE
ASSASSINS**

234th novel in the exciting LONGARM series
from Jove

Coming in June!